SO-ABJ-383

The Terrestrial (and other) Joy-Girls Were Waiting

"The feast ends," F'Kau-Kau-Kau said. "Now you and I, Retief, must straddle the Council Stool."

"I'll be honored, Your Admirableness," Retief said. "I must inform my colleagues."

F'Kau-Kau-Kau emptied a squat tumbler of pink beer. "I'll treat with you, Retief, as viceroy, since as you say your king is old and the space between worlds is far. But there shall be no scheming underlings privy to our dealings." He grinned a Yill grin. "Afterwards we shall carouse, Retief. The Council Stool is hard, and the waiting handmaidens delectable; this makes for quick agreement."

Retief smiled. "The Admirable speaks wisdom."

KEITH LAUMER

RETIEF: ENVOY TO NEW WORLDS

BAEN BOOKS

RETIEF: ENVOY TO NEW WORLDS

This is a work of fiction. All the characters and events portrayed in this book are fictional, and any resemblance to real people or incidents is purely coincidental.

Copyright © 1963 by Keith Laumer

All rights reserved, including the right to reproduce this book or portions thereof in any form.

A Baen Book

Baen Publishing Enterprises
260 Fifth Avenue
New York, N.Y. 10001

First Baen printing, April 1987

ISBN: 0-671-65635-X

Cover art by Wayne Barlowe

Printed in the United States of America

Distributed by
SIMON & SCHUSTER
1230 Avenue of the Americas
New York, N.Y. 10020

To Dr. LEON WRIGHT
a genuine diplomat

CONTENTS

Protocol

"... into the chaotic Galactic political scene of the post-Concordiat era, the CDT emerged to carry forward the ancient diplomatic tradition as a great supra-national organization dedicated to the contravention of war.[1] As mediators of disputes among Terrestrial-settled worlds and advocates of Terrestrial interests in contacts with alien cultures, Corps diplomats, trained in the chanceries of innumerable defunct bureaucracies, displayed an encyclopedic grasp of the nuances of Estra-Terrestrial mores as set against the labyrinthine socio-politico-economic Galactic context. Never was the virtuosity of a senior Corps diplomat more brilliantly displayed than in Ambassador Spradley's negotiation of the awkward Sirenian Question. . . ."*

—extract from the *Official History of the Corps Diplomatique*, Vol I, reel 2. Solarian Press, New New York, 479 A. E. (AD 2940)

---

1) Cf. the original colorful language: "maintenance of a state of tension short of actual conflict." See CDT File 178/b/491, col. VII, spool 12; 745 mm (code 2g).

IN THE GLOOM of the squat, mud-colored reception building, the Counselor, two First Secretaries, and the senior Attachés gathered around the plump figure of Ambassador Spradley, their ornate diplomatic uniforms bright in the vast gloomy room. The Ambassador glanced at his finger watch impatiently.

"Ben, are you quite certain our arrival time was made clear?"

Second Secretary Magnan nodded emphatically. "I stressed the point, Mr. Ambassador. I communicated with Mr. T'Cai-Cai just before the lighter broke orbit, and I specifically emphasized— "

"I hope you didn't appear truculent, Mr. Magnan," the Ambassador cut in sharply.

"No indeed, Mr. Ambassador. I merely—"

"You're sure there's no VIP room here?" The Ambassador glanced around the cavernous room. "Curious that not even chairs have been provided."

"If you'd care to sit on one of those crates, I'll use my hanky—"

"Certainly not." The Ambassador looked at his watch again and cleared his throat.

"I may as well make use of these few moments to outline our approach for the more junior members of the staff. It's vital that the entire mission work in harmony in the presentation of the image. We Terrestrials are a kindly, peace-loving race." The Ambassador smiled in a kindly, peace-loving way.

"We seek only reasonable division of spheres of influence with the Yill." He spread his hands, looking reasonable.

"We are a people of high culture, ethical, sincere."

The smile was replaced abruptly by pursed lips. "We'll start by asking for the entire Sirenian System, and settle for half. We'll establish a foothold on all the choicer worlds and, with shrewd handling, in a decade we'll be in a position to assert a wider claim." The Ambassador glanced around. "If there are no questions . . ."

Jame Retief, Vice-Consul and Third Secretary in the Corps Diplomatique and junior member of the Terrestrial Embassy to Yill, stepped forward.

"Since we hold the prior claim to the system, why don't we put all our cards on the table to start with? Perhaps if we dealt frankly with the Yill, it would pay us in the long run."

Ambassador Spradley blinked up at the younger man. Beside him, Magnan cleared his throat in the silence.

"Vice-Consul Retief merely means—"

"I'm capable of interpreting Mr. Retief's remark," Spradley snapped. He assumed a fatherly expression. "Young man, you're new to the service. You haven't yet learned the team play, the give-and-take of diplomacy. I shall expect you to observe closely the work of the experienced negotiators of the mission, learn the importance of subtlety. Excessive reliance on direct methods might tend in time to attenuate the rôle of the professional diplomat. I shudder to contemplate the consequences."

Spradley turned back to his senior staff members. Retief strolled across to a glass-panelled door and glanced into the room beyond. Several dozen tall grey-skinned Yill lounged in deep couches, sipping lavender drinks from slender glass tubes. Black-tunicked servants moved about inconspicuously, offering trays. Retief watched as a party of brightly-dressed Yill moved toward a wide entrance door. One of the party, a tall male, made to step before another, who raised a hand languidly, fist clenched. The first Yill stepped back and placed his hands on top of his head with a nod. Both Yill continued to smile and chatter as they passed through the door.

Retief rejoined the Terrestrial delegation, grouped around a mound of rough crates stacked on the bare concrete floor, as a small leather-skinned Yill came up.

"I am P'Toi. Come thiss way . . ." He motioned. The Terrestrials moved off, Ambassador Spradley in the lead. As the portly diplomat reached the door, the Yill guide darted ahead, shouldering him aside, then hesitated, waiting. The Ambassador almost glared, then remembered the image. He smiled, beckoning the Yill ahead. The Yill muttered in the native language, stared about, then passed through the door. The Terran party followed.

"I'd like to know what that fellow was saying," Magnan said, overtaking the Ambassador. "The way he jostled your Excellency was disgraceful."

A number of Yill waited on the pavement outside the building. As Spradley approached the luxurious open car waiting at the curb, they closed ranks, blocking his way. He drew himself up, opened his mouth—then closed it with a snap.

"The very idea," Magnan said, trotting at Spradley's heels as he stalked back to rejoin the staff, now looking around uncertainly. "One would think these persons weren't aware of the courtesies due a Chief of Mission."

"They're not aware of the courtesies due an apprentice sloat skinner!" Spradley snapped. Around the Terrestrials, the Yill milled nervously, muttering in the native tongue.

"Where has our confounded interpreter betaken himself?" The Ambassador barked. "I daresay they're plotting openly. . . ."

"A pity we have to rely on a native interpreter."

"Had I known we'd meet this rather uncouth reception," the Ambassador said stiffly, "I would have audited the language personally, of course, during the voyage out."

"Oh, no criticism intended, of course, Mr. Ambassador," Magnan said hastily. "Heavens, who would have thought—"

Retief stepped up beside the Ambassador.

"Mr. Ambassador," he said. "I—"

"Later, young man," the Ambassador snapped. He beckoned to the Counselor, and the two moved off, heads together.

A bluish sun gleamed in a dark sky. Retief
watched his breath form a frosty cloud in the chill
air. A broad hard-wheeled vehicle pulled up to the
platform. The Yill gestured the Terran party to the
gaping door at the rear, then stood back, waiting.

Retief looked curiously at the grey-painted van.
The legend written on its side in alien symbols
seemed to read "egg nog." Unfortunately he hadn't
had time to learn the script too, on the trip out.
Perhaps later he would have a chance to tell the
Ambassador he could interpret for the mission.

The Ambassador entered the vehicle, the other
Terrestrials following. It was as bare of seats as the
Terminal building. What appeared to be a defunct
electronic chassis lay in the center of the floor,
amid a litter of paper and a purple and yellow sock
designed for a broad Yill foot. Retief glanced back.
The Yill were talking excitedly. None of them
entered the car. The door was closed, and the
Terrans braced themselves under the low roof as
the engine started up with a whine of worn turbos,
and the van moved off.

It was an uncomfortable ride. The unsprung
wheels hammered uneven cobblestones. Retief put
out an arm as the vehicle rounded a corner, caught
the Ambassador as he staggered off-balance. The
Ambassador glared at him, settled his heavy tri-
corner hat, and stood stiffly until the car lurched
again.

Retief stooped, trying to see out through the
single dusty window. They seemed to be in a wide
street lined with low buildings. They passed through
a massive gate, up a ramp, and stopped. The door
opened. Retief looked out at a blank grey facade,
broken by tiny windows at irregular intervals. A

scarlet vehicle was drawn up ahead, the Yill reception committee emerging from it. Through its wide windows Retief saw rich upholstery and caught a glimpse of glasses clamped to a tiny bar.

P'Toi, the Yill interpreter, came forward, gesturing to a small door in the grey wall. Magnan scurried ahead to open it and held it for the Ambassador. As he stepped to it a Yill thrust himself ahead and hesitated. Ambassador Spradley drew himself up, glaring. Then he twisted his mouth into a frozen smile and stepped aside. The Yill looked at each other, then filed through the door.

Retief was the last to enter. As he stepped inside a black-clad servant slipped past him, pulled the lid from a large box by the door and dropped in a paper tray heaped with refuse. There were alien symbols in flaking paint on the box. They seemed, Retief noticed, to spell "egg nog."

The shrill pipes and whining reeds had been warming up for an hour when Retief emerged from his cubicle and descended the stairs to the banquet hall. Standing by the open doors he lit a slender cigar and watched through narrowed eyes as obsequious servants in black flitted along the low wide corridor, carrying laden trays into the broad room, arranging settings on a great four-sided table forming a hollow square that almost filled the room. Rich brocades were spread across the center of the side nearest the door, flanked by heavily decorated white cloths. Beyond, plain white extended down the two sides to the far board, where metal dishes were arranged on the bare table top. A richly dressed Yill approached, stepped aside to allow a servant to pass and entered the room.

Retief turned at the sound of Terran voices behind him. The Ambassador came up, trailed by two diplomats. He glanced at Retief, adjusted his ruff and looked into the banquet hall.

"Apparently we're to be kept waiting again," he snapped. "After having been informed at the outset that the Yill have no intention of yielding an inch, one almost wonders . . ."

"Mr. Ambassador," Retief said. "Have you noticed—"

"However," Ambassador Spradley said, eyeing Retief, "A seasoned diplomatist must take these little snubs in stride. In the end—ah there, Magnan . . ." He turned away, talking.

Somewhere a gong clanged. In a moment the corridor was filled with chattering Yill who moved past the group of Terrestrials into the banquet hall. P'Toi, the Yill interpreter, came up, raised a hand.

"Waitt heere . . ."

More Yill filed into the dining room, taking their places. A pair of helmeted guards approached and waved the Terrestrials back. An immense greyjowled Yill waddled to the doors, ropes of jewels clashing softly, and passed through, followed by more guards.

"The Chief of State," Retief heard Magnan say. "The Admirable F'Kau-Kau-Kau."

"I have yet to present my credentials," Ambassador Spradley said. "One expects some latitude in the observances of protocol, but I confess . . ." He wagged his head.

The Yill interpreter spoke up.

"You now whill lhie on yourr intesstinss and creep to fesstive board there." He pointed across the room.

"Intestines?" Ambassador Spradley looked about wildly.

"Mr. P'Toi means our stomachs, I wouldn't wonder," Magnan said. "He just wants us to lie down and crawl to our seats, Mr. Ambassador."

"What the devil are you grinning at, you idiot?" the Ambassador snapped.

Magnan's face fell.

Spradley glanced down at the medals across his paunch.

"This is . . . I've never . . ."

"Homage to godss," the interpreter said.

"Oh-oh—religion," someone said.

"Well, if it's a matter of religious beliefs . . ." The Ambassador looked around dubiously.

"Actually, it's only a couple of hundred feet," Magnan said.

Retief stepped up to P'Toi.

"His Excellency, the Terrestrial Ambassador will not crawl," he said clearly.

"Here, young man, I said nothing—"

"Not to crawl?" The interpreter wore an unreadable Yill expression.

"It is against our religion," Retief said.

"Againsst?"

"We are votaries of the Snake Goddess," Retief said. "It is a sacrilege to crawl." He brushed past the interpreter and marched toward the distant table. The others followed.

Puffing, the Ambassador came to Retief's side as they approached the dozen empty stools on the far

side of the square opposite the brocaded position
of the Admirable F'Kau-Kau-Kau.

"Mr. Retief, kindly see me after this affair," he
hissed. "In the meantime, I hope you will restrain
any further rash impulses. Let me remind you *I*
am Chief of Mission here."

Magnan came up from behind.

"Let me add my congratulations, Retief," he
said. "That was fast thinking."

"Are you out of your mind, Magnan?" the Ambassador barked. "I am extremely displeased."

"Why," Magnan stuttered, "I was speaking sar-
castically, of course, Mr. Ambassador. Naturally I,
too, was taken aback by his presumption."

The Terrestrials took their places, Retief at the
end. The table before them was of bare green
wood, with an array of shallow pewter dishes upon
it.

The Yill at the table, some in plain grey, others
in black, eyed them silently. There was a constant
stir among them as one or another rose and disappeared and others sat down. The pipes and reeds
of the orchestra were shrilling furiously and the
susurration of Yillian conversation from the other
tables rose ever higher in competition. A tall Yill
in black was at the Ambassador's side now. The
nearby Yill all fell silent as the servant ladled a
whitish soup into the largest of the bowls before
the Terrestrial envoy. The interpreter hovered,
watching.

"That's quite enough," Ambassador Spradley said,
as the bowl overflowed. The Yill servant dribbled
more of the soup into the bowl. It welled out
across the table top.

"Kindly serve the other members of my staff,"

the Ambassador commanded. The interpreter said
something in a low voice. The servant moved
hesitantly to the next stool and ladled more
soup.

Retief watched, listening to the whispers around
him. The Yill at the table were craning now to
watch. The servant was ladling the soup rapidly,
rolling his eyes sideways. He came to Retief and
reached out with the full ladle for the bowl.

"No," Retief said.

The servant hesitated.

"None for me," Retief said.

The interpreter came up, motioned to the servant, who reached again, ladle brimming.

"I don't want any!" Retief said, his voice distinct
in the sudden hush. He stared at the interpreter,
who stared back for a moment, then waved the
servant away and moved on.

"Mr. Retief," a voice hissed. Retief looked down
the table. The Ambassador was leaning forward,
glaring at him, his face a mottled crimson.

"I'm warning you, Mr. Retief," he said hoarsely.
"I've eaten sheep's eyes in the Sudan, *ka swe* in
Burma, hundred-year *cug* on Mars, and everything else that has been placed before me in the
course of my diplomatic career, and by the holy
relics of Saint Ignatz, you'll do the same!" He
snatched up a spoon-like utensil and dipped it into
his bowl.

"Don't eat that, Mr. Ambassador," Retief said.

The Ambassador stared, eyes wide. He opened
his mouth, guiding the spoon toward it.

Retief stood, gripped the table under its edge,
and heaved. The immense wooden slab rose and
tilted; dishes crashed to the floor. The table fol-

lowed with a ponderous slam. Milky soup splattered across the terrazzo; a couple of odd bowls rolled clattering across the room. Cries rang out from the Yill, mingling with a strangled yell from Ambassador Spradley.

Retief walked past the wild-eyed members of the mission to the sputtering chief. "Mr. Ambassador," he said. "I'd like—"

"You'd like! I'll break you, you young hoodlum! Do you realize—"

"Pleass . . ." The interpreter stood at Retief's side.

"My apologies," Ambassador Spradley said, mopping his forehead. "My profound—"

"Be quiet," Retief said.

"Wh-what?!"

"Don't apologize," Retief said.

P'Toi was beckoning. "Please, arll come."

Retief turned and followed him.

The portion of the table they were ushered to was covered with an embroidered white cloth, set with thin porcelain dishes. The Yill already seated there rose, amid babbling and moved down to make room for the Terrestrials. The black-clad Yill at the end table closed ranks to fill the vacant seats. Retief sat down, finding Magnan at his side.

"What's going on here?" the Second Secretary said.

"They were giving us dog food," Retief said. "I overheard a Yill. They seated us at the servants' section of the table."

"You mean you understand the language?"

"I learned it on the way out—enough, at least—"

The music burst out with a clangorous fanfare, and a throng of jugglers, dancers, and acrobats poured into the center of the hollow square, frantically juggling, dancing, and back-flipping. Servants swarmed, heaping mounds of fragrant food on the plates of Yill and Terrestrials alike, pouring pale purple liquor into slender glasses. Retief sampled the Yill food. It was delicious. Conversation was impossible in the din. He watched the gaudy display and ate heartily.

Retief leaned back, grateful for the lull in the music. The last of the dishes were whisked away, and more glasses filled. The exhausted entertainers stopped to pick up the thick square coins the diners threw. Retief sighed. It had been a rare feast.

"Retief," Magnan said in the comparative quiet. "What were you saying about dog food as the music came up?"

Retief looked at him. "Haven't you noticed the pattern, Mr. Magnan? The series of deliberate affronts?"

"Deliberate affronts! Just a minute, Retief. They're uncouth, yes, crowding into doorways and that sort of thing. But . . ." He looked at Retief uncertainly.

"They herded us into a baggage warehouse at the terminal. Then they hauled us here in a garbage truck."

"Garbage truck!"

"Only symbolic, of course. They ushered us in the tradesmen's entrance, and assigned us cubicles in the servants' wing. Then we were seated with the coolie-class sweepers at the bottom of the table."

"You must be mistaken! I mean, after all, we're

the Terrestrial delegation; surely these Yill must realize our power."

"Precisely, Mr. Magnan. But—"

With a clang of cymbals, the musicians launched a renewed assault. Six tall, helmeted Yill sprang into the center of the floor, paired off in a wild performance, half dance, half combat. Magnan pulled at Retief's sleeve, his mouth moving. Retief shook his head. No one could talk against a Yill orchestra in full cry. Retief sampled a bright red wine and watched the show.

There was a flurry of action, and two of the dancers stumbled and collapsed, their partner-opponents whirling away to pair off again, describe the elaborate pre-combat ritual, and abruptly, set to, dulled sabres clashing—and two more Yill were down, stunned. It was a violent dance. Retief watched, the drink forgotten.

The last two Yill approached and retreated, whirled, bobbed, and spun, feinted and postured. And then one was slipping, going down, helmet awry, and the other, a giant, muscular Yill, spun away, whirled in a mad skirl of pipes as coins showered—then froze before a gaudy table, raised the sabre, and slammed it down in a resounding blow across the gay cloth before a lace-and-bow-bedecked Yill. The music stopped with a ringing clash of cymbals.

In utter silence the dancer-fighter stared across the table. With a shout the seated Yill leaped up and raised a clenched fist. The dancer bowed his head, spread his hands on his helmet and resumed his dance as the music blared anew. The berib-boned Yill waved a hand negligently, flung a hand-ful of coins across the floor, and sat down.

Now the dancer stood rigid before the brocaded table—and the music chopped off short as the sabre slammed down before a heavy Yill in ornate metallic coils. The challenged Yill rose, raised a fist, and the other ducked his head, putting his hands on his helmet. Coins rolled, and the dancer moved on.

He circled the broad floor, sabre twirling, arms darting in an intricate symbolism. Then suddenly he was towering before Retief, sabre above his head. The music cut, and in the startling instanteous silence, the heavy sabre whipped over and down with an explosive concussion that set dishes dancing on the table-top.

The Yill's eyes held on Retief's. In the silence Magnan tittered drunkenly. Retief pushed back his stool.

"Steady, my boy," Ambassador Spradley called. Retief stood, the Yill topping his six-foot-three by an inch. In a motion too quick to follow Retief reached for the sabre, twitched it from the Yill's grasp, swung it in a whistling arc. The Yill ducked, sprang back and snatched up a sabre dropped by another dancer.

"Someone stop the madman!" Spradley howled.

Retief leaped across the table, sending fragile dishes spinning.

The other danced back, and only then did the orchestra spring to life with a screech and a mad tattoo of high-pitched drums.

Making no attempt to follow the weaving pattern of the Yill bolero, Retief pressed the Yill, fending off vicious cuts with the blunt weapon, chopping back relentlessly. Left hand on hip, Retief matched blow for blow, driving the other back.

Abruptly the Yill abandoned the double role. Dancing forgotten, he settled down in earnest, cutting, thrusting, parrying. Now the two stood toe to toe, sabres clashing in a lightning exchange. The Yill gave a step, two, then rallied, drove Retief back, back—

Retief feinted, laid a hearty whack across the grey skull. The Yill stumbled, his sabre clattered to the floor. Retief stepped aside as the Yill wavered past him and crashed to the floor.

The orchestra fell silent in a descending wail of reeds. Retief drew a deep breath and wiped his forehead.

"Come back here, you young fool!" Spradley called hoarsely.

Retief hefted the sabre, turned, eyed the brocade-draped table. He started across the floor. The Yill sat as if paralyzed.

"Retief, no!" Spradley yelped.

Retief walked directly to the Admirable F'Kau-Kau-Kau, stopped, raised the sabre.

"Not the Chief of State," someone in the Terrestrial Mission groaned.

Retief whipped the sabre down. The dull blade split the heavy brocade and cleaved the hardwood table. There was utter silence.

The Admirable F'Kau-Kau-Kau rose, seven feet of obese grey Yill. His broad face expressionless to the Terran eye, he raised a fist like a jewel-studded ham.

Retief stood rigid for a long moment. Then, gracefully, he inclined his head and placed his finger tips on his temples. Behind him there was a clatter as Ambassador Spradley collapsed. Then the Admirable F'Kau-Kau-Kau cried out, reached across the table to embrace the Terrestrial, and the orchestra went mad. Grey hands helped Retief across the table, stools were pushed aside to make room at F'Kau-Kau-Kau's side. Retief sat, took a tall flagon of coal-black brandy pressed on him by his neighbor, clashed glasses with The Admirable, and drank.

"The feast ends," F'Kau-Kau-Kau said. "Now you and I, Retief, must straddle the Council Stool."

"I'll be honored, Your Admirableness," Retief said. "I must inform my colleagues."

"Colleagues?" F'Kau-Kau-Kau said. "It is for chiefs to parley. Who shall speak for a king while he yet has tongue for talk?"

"The Yill way is wise," Retief said.

F'Kau-Kau-Kau emptied a squat tumbler of pink beer. "I'll treat with you, Retief, as viceroy, since as you say your king is old and the space between worlds is far. But there shall be no scheming underlings privy to our dealings." He grinned a Yill grin. "Afterwards we shall carouse, Retief. The Council Stool is hard, and the waiting handmaidens delectable; this makes for quick agreement."

Retief smiled. "The Admirable speaks wisdom."

"Of course, a being prefers wenches of his own kind," F'Kau-Kau-Kau said. He belched. "The Ministry of Culture has imported several Terrestrial joy-girls, said to be top-notch specimens. As least they have very fat watchamacallits."

"Your Admirableness is most considerate," Retief said.

"Let us to it then, Retief. I may hazard a tumble with one of your Terries, myself. I fancy an occasional perversion." F'Kau-Kau-Kau dug an elbow into Retief's side and bellowed with laughter.

As Retief crossed to the door at F'Kau-Kau-Kau's side, Ambassador Spradley glowered from behind the plain tablecloth. "Retief," he called, "kindly excuse yourself. I wish a word with you." His voice was icy. Magnan stood behind him, goggling.

"Forgive my apparent rudeness, Mr. Ambassador," said Retief. "I don't have time to explain now—"

"Rudeness!" Spradley yipped. "Don't have time, eh? Let me tell you—"

"Please lower your voice, Mr. Ambassador," Retief said. "The situation is still delicate."

Spradley quivered, his mouth open. He found his voice, "You—you—"

"Silence!" Retief snapped. Spradley looked up at Retief's face, staring for a moment into Retief's grey eyes. He closed his mouth and swallowed.

"The Yill seem to have gotten the impression I'm in charge," Retief said. "We'll have to maintain the deception."

"But—but—" Spradley stuttered. Then he straightened. "That is the last straw," he whispered hoarsely. "*I* am the Terrestrial Ambassador Extraordinary and Minister Plenipotentiary. Magnan has told me that we've been studiedly and repeatedly insulted, since the moment of our arrival; kept waiting in baggage rooms, transported in refuse lorries, herded about with servants, offered swill at the table. Now I, and my senior staff, are left cooling our heels, without so much as an audience, while this—this multiple Kau person hobnobs with—with—"

Spradley's voice broke. "I may have been a trifle hasty, Retief, in attempting to restrain you. Slighting the native gods and dumping the banquet table are rather extreme measures, but your resentment was perhaps partially justified. I am prepared to be lenient with you." He fixed a choleric eye on Retief.

"I am walking out of this meeting, Mr. Retief. I'll take no more of these personal—"

"That's enough," Retief said sharply. "We're keeping The Admirable waiting."

Spradley's face purpled.

Magnan found his voice. "What are you going to do, Retief?"

"I'm going to handle the negotiation," Retief said. He handed Magnan his empty glass. "Now go sit down and work on the Image."

At his desk in the VIP suite aboard the orbiting Corps vessel, Ambassador Spradley pursed his lips and looked severely at Vice-Consul Retief.

"Further," he said, "you have displayed a complete lack of understanding of Corps discipline, the respect due a senior officer, even the basic courtesies. Your aggravated displays of temper, ill-timed outbursts of violence, and almost incredible arrogance in the assumption of authority make your further retention as an Officer-Agent of the Corps Diplomatique Terrestrienne impossible. It will therefore be my unhappy duty to recommend your immediate—"

There was a muted buzz from the communicator. The Ambassador cleared his throat.

"Well?"

"A signal from Sector HQ, Mr. Ambassador," a voice said.

"Well, read it," Spradley snapped. "Skip the preliminaries . . ."

"Congratulations on the unprecedented success of your mission. The articles of agreement transmitted by you embody a most favorable resolution of the difficult Sirenian situation, and will form the basis of continued amicable relations between the Terrestrial States and the Yill Empire. To you and your staff, full credit is due for a job well done. Signed, Deputy Assistant Secretary Sternwheeler."

Spradley cut off the voice impatiently. He shuffled papers, then eyed Retief sharply.

"Superficially, of course, an uninitiated observer might leap to the conclusion that the ah . . . results that were produced in spite of these . . . ah . . . irregularities justify the latter." The Ambassador smiled a sad, wise smile. "This is far from the case," he said. "I—"

The communicator burped softly.

"Confound it." Spradley muttered. "Yes?"

"Mr. T'Cai-Cai has arrived," the voice said. "Shall I—"

"Send him in, at once." Spradley glanced at Retief. "Only a two-syllable man, but I shall attempt to correct these false impressions, make some amends . . ."

The two Terrestrials waited silently until the Yill Protocol chief tapped at the door.

"I hope," the Ambassador said, "that you will resist the impulse to take advantage of your unusual position." He looked at the door. "Come in."

T'Cai-Cai stepped into the room, glanced at Spradley, then turned to greet Retief in voluble

Yill. He rounded the desk to the Ambassador's chair, motioned him from it, and sat down.

"I have a surprise for you, Retief," he said in Terran. "I myself have made use of the teaching machine you so kindly lent us."

"That's good," Retief said. "I'm sure Mr. Spradley will be interested in hearing what we have to say."

"Never mind," the Yill said. "I am here only socially." He looked around the room.

"So plainly you decorate your chamber; but it has a certain austere charm." He laughed a Yill laugh.

"Oh, you are a strange breed, you Terrestrials. You surprised us all. You know, one hears such outlandish stories. I tell you in confidence, we had expected you to be overpushes."

"Pushovers," Spradley said tonelessly.

"Such restraint! What pleasure you gave to those of us, like myself of course, who appreciated your grasp of protocol. Such finesse! How subtly you appeared to ignore each overture, while neatly avoiding actual contamination. I can tell you, there were those who thought—poor fools—that you had no grasp of etiquette. How gratified we were, we professionals, who could appreciate your virtuosity—when you placed matters on a comfortable basis by spurning the cats'-meat. It was sheer pleasure then, waiting, to see what form your compliment would take."

The Yill offered orange cigars, then stuffed one in his nostril.

"I confess even I had not hoped that you would honor our Admirable so signally. Oh, it is a pleasure to deal with fellow professionals, who understand the meaning of protocol."

Ambassador Spradley made a choking sound.

"This fellow has caught a chill," T'Cai-Cai said. He eyed Spradley dubiously. "Step back, my man, I am highly susceptible.

"There is one bit of business I shall take pleasure in attending to, my dear Retief," T'Cai-Cai went on. He drew a large paper from his reticule. "His Admirableness is determined that none other than yourself shall be accredited here. I have here my government's exequatur confirming you as Terrestrial Consul-General to Yill. We shall look forward to your prompt return."

Retief looked at Spradley.

"I'm sure the Corps will agree," he said.

"Then I shall be going," T'Cai-Cai said. He stood up. "Hurry back to us, Retief. There is much that I would show you of the great Empire of Yill." He winked a Yill wink.

"Together, Retief, we shall see many high and splendid things."

Sealed Orders

*. . . In the face of the multitudinous threats
to the peace arising naturally from the complex
Galactic situation, the polished techniques de-
vised by Corps theoreticians proved their worth
in a thousand difficult confrontations. Even
anonymous junior officers, armed with brief-
cases containing detailed instructions, were
able to soothe troubled waters with the skill
of experienced negotiators. A case in point was
Consul Passwyn's incisive handling of the Jaq-
Terrestrial contretemps at Adobe . . .*

Vol. II, reel 91 480 A. E. (AD 2941)

"IT's TRUE," Consul Passwyn said, "I requested assignment as Principle Officer at a small post. But I had in mind one of those charming resort worlds, with only an occasional visa problem, or perhaps a distressed spaceman or two a year. Instead, I'm zoo-keeper to these confounded settlers, and not for one world, mind you, but eight." He stared glumly at Vice-Consul Retief.

"Still," Retief said, "it gives an opportunity for travel."

"Travel!" the Consul barked. "I hate travel. Here in this backwater system particularly. . . ." He paused, blinked at Retief, and cleared his throat. "Not that a bit of travel isn't an excellent thing for a junior officer. Marvelous experience."

He turned to the wall-screen and pressed a button. A system triagram appeared: eight luminous green dots arranged around a larger disc representing the primary. Passwyn picked up a pointer, indicating the innermost planet.

"The situation on Adobe is nearing crisis. The confounded settlers—a mere handful of them—have managed, as usual, to stir up trouble with an intelligent indigenous life form, the Jaq. I can't think why they bother, merely for a few oases among the endless deserts. However, I have, at last, received authorization from Sector Headquarters to take certain action."

He swung back to face Retief. "I'm sending you in to handle the situation, Retief—under sealed orders." He picked up a fat, buff envelope. "A pity they didn't see fit to order the Terrestrial settlers out weeks ago, as I suggested. Now it's too late. I'm expected to produce a miracle—a rapprochement between Terrestrial and Jaq and a division of territory. It's idiotic. However, failure would look very bad in my record, so I shall expect results." He passed the buff envelope across to Retief.

"I understood that Adobe was uninhabited," Retief said, "until the Terrestrial settlers arrived."

"Apparently that was an erroneous impression. The Jaq are there." Passwyn fixed Retief with a watery eye. "You'll follow your instructions to the letter. In a delicate situation such as this, there must be no impulsive, impromptu element introduced. This approach has been worked out in detail at Sector; you need merely implement it. Is that entirely clear?"

"Has anyone at Headquarters ever visited Adobe?"

"Of course not. They all hate travel too. If there are no other questions, you'd best be on your way. The mail run departs the dome in less than an hour."

"What's this native life form like?" Retief asked, getting to his feet.

"When you get back," said Passwyn, "you tell me."

The mail pilot, a leathery veteran with quarter-inch whiskers, spat toward a stained corner of the compartment, and leaned close to the screen.

"They's shootin' goin' on down there," he said. "Them white puffs over the edge of the desert."

"I'm supposed to be preventing the war," said Retief. "It looks like I'm a little late."

The pilot's head snapped around. "War?" he yelped. "Nobody told me they was a war goin' on on 'Dobe. If that's what that is, I'm gettin' out of here."

"Hold on," said Retief. "I've got to get down. They won't shoot at you."

"They shore won't, sonny. I ain't givin' 'em the chance." He reached for the console and started punching keys. Retief reached out, catching his wrist.

"Maybe you didn't hear me. I said I've got to get down."

The pilot plunged against the restraint and swung a punch that Retief blocked casually. "Are you nuts?" the pilot screeched. "They's plenty shootin' goin' on fer me to see it fifty miles out."

"The mails must go through, you know."

"I ain't no consarned postman. If you're so dead set on gettin' killed—take the skiff. I'll tell 'em to pick up the remains next trip—if the shootin's over."

"You're a pal. I'll take your offer."

The pilot jumped to the lifeboat hatch and cy-

cled it open. "Get in. We're closin' fast. Them
birds might take it into their heads to lob one this
way."

Retief crawled into the narrow cockpit of the
skiff. The pilot ducked out of sight, came back,
and handed Retief a heavy old-fashioned power
pistol. "Long as you're goin' in, might as well take
this."

"Thanks." Retief shoved the pistol in his belt. "I
hope you're wrong."

"I'll see they pick you up when the shootin's
over—one way or another."

The hatch clanked shut; a moment later there
was a jar as the skiff dropped away, followed by
heavy buffeting in the backwash from the departing mail boat. Retief watched the tiny screen, his
hands on the manual controls. He was dropping
rapidly: forty miles, thirty-nine . . .

At five miles, Retief threw the light skiff into
maximum deceleration. Crushed back in the padded seat, he watched the screen and corrected the
course minutely. The planetary surface was rushing up with frightening speed. Retief shook his
head and kicked in the emergency retro-drive.
Points of light arced up from the planet face below. If they were ordinary chemical warheads the
skiff's meteor screens should handle them. The
screen on the instrument panel flashed brilliant
white, then went dark. The skiff leaped and flipped
on its back; smoke filling the tiny compartment.
There was a series of shocks, a final bone-shaking
concussion, then stillness broken by the ping of
hot metal contracting.

Coughing, Retief disengaged himself from the
shock-webbing, groped underfoot for the hatch,

and wrenched it open. A wave of hot jungle air struck him. He lowered himself to a bed of shattered foliage, got to his feet . . . and dropped flat as a bullet whined past his ear.

He lay listening. Stealthy movements were audible from the left. He inched his way forward and made the shelter of a broad-boled dwarf tree. Somewhere a song lizard burbled. Whining insects circled, scented alien life, and buzzed off. There was another rustle of foliage from the underbrush five yards away. A bush quivered, then a low bough dipped. Retief edged back around the trunk and eased down behind a fallen log. A stocky man in a grimy leather shirt and shorts appeared, moving cautiously, a pistol in his hand.

As he passed, Retief rose, leaped the log, and tackled him. They went down together. The man gave one short yell, then struggled in silence. Retief flipped him onto his back, raised a fist—

"Hey!" the settler yelled. "You're as human as I am!"

"Maybe I'll look better after a shave," said Retief. "What's the idea of shooting at me?"

"Lemme up—my name's Potter. Sorry 'bout that. I figured it was a Flap-jack boat; looks just like 'em. I took a shot when I saw something move; didn't know it was a Terrestrial. Who are you? What you doin' here? We're pretty close to the edge of the oasis. That's Flap-jack country over there." He waved a hand toward the north, where the desert lay.

"I'm glad you're a poor shot. Some of those missiles were too close for comfort."

"Missiles, eh? Must be Flap-jack artillery. We got nothin' like that."

"I heard there was a full-fledged war brewing," said Retief. "I didn't expect—"

"Good!" Potter said. "We figured a few of you boys from Ivory would be joining up when you heard. You from Ivory?"

"Yes. I'm—"

"Hey, you must be Lemuel's cousin. Good night! I pretty near made a bad mistake. Lemuel's a tough man to explain anything to."

"I'm—"

"Keep your head down. These damn Flap-jacks have got some wicked hand weapons. Come on . . ." He began crawling through the brush. Retief followed. They crossed two hundred yards of rough country before Potter got to his feet, took out a soggy bandana, and mopped his face.

"You move good for a city man. I thought you folks on Ivory just sat under those domes and read dials. But I guess bein' Lemuel's cousin—"

"As a matter of fact—"

"Have to get you some real clothes, though. Those city duds don't stand up on 'Dobe."

Retief looked down at his charred, torn, sweat-soaked powder-blue blazer and slacks, the informal uniform of a Third Secretary and Vice-Consul in the Corps Diplomatique Terrestrienne.

"This outfit seemed pretty rough-and-ready back home," he said. "But I guess leather has its points."

"Let's get on back to camp. We'll just about make it by sundown. And look, don't say nothin' to Lemuel about me thinkin' you were a Flap-jack."

"I won't; but—"

Potter was on his way, loping off up a gentle

slope. Retief pulled off the sodden blazer, dropped it over a bush, added his string tie, and followed Potter.

"We're damn glad you're here, mister," said a fat man with two revolvers belted across his paunch. "We can use every man. We're in bad shape. We ran into the Flap-jacks three months ago and we haven't made a smart move since. First, we thought they were a native form we hadn't run into before. Fact is, one of the boys shot one, think' it was fair game. I guess that was the start of it." He paused to stir the fire.

"And then a bunch of 'em hit Swazey's farm here. Killed two of his cattle, and pulled back," he said.

"We figure they thought the cows were people," said Swazey. "They were out for revenge."

"How could anybody think a cow was folks," another man put in. "They don't look nothin' like—"

"Don't be so dumb, Bert," said Swazey. "They'd never seen Terries before; they know better now."

Bert chuckled. "Sure do. We showed 'em the next time, didn't we, Potter? Got four—"

"They walked right up to my place a couple days after the first time," Swazey said. "We were ready for 'em. Peppered 'em good. They cut and run—"

"Flopped, you mean. Ugliest-lookin' critters you ever saw. Look just like an old piece of dirty blanket humpin' around."

"It's been goin' on this way ever since. They raid and then we raid. But lately they've been bringin' some big stuff into it. They've got some kind of pint-sized airships and automatic rifles.

We've lost four men now and a dozen more in the freezer, waiting for the med ship. We can't afford it. The colony's got less than three hundred able-bodied men."

"But we're hangin' onto our farms," said Potter. "All these oases are old sea-beds—a mile deep, solid topsoil. And there's a couple of hundred others we haven't touched yet. The Flap-jacks won't get 'em while there's a man alive."

"The whole system needs the food we can raise," Bert said. "These farms we're tryin' to start won't be enough but they'll help."

"We been yellin' for help to the CDT, over on Ivory," said Potter. "But you know these Embassy stooges."

"We heard they were sendin' some kind of bureaucrat in here to tell us to get out and give the oasis to the Flap-jacks," said Swazey. He tightened his mouth. "We're waitin' for him. . . ."

"Meanwhile we got reinforcements comin' up. We put out the word back home; we all got relatives on Ivory and Verde—"

"Shut up, you damn fool!" a deep voice grated.

"Lemuel!" Potter said. "Nobody else could sneak up on us like that—"

"If I'd been a Flap-jack, I'd of et you alive," the newcomer said, moving into the ring of the fire. He was a tall, broad-faced man in grimy leather. He eyed Retief.

"Who's that?"

"What do ya mean?" Potter spoke in the silence. "He's your cousin."

"He ain't no cousin of mine," Lemuel said. He stepped to Retief.

"Who you spyin' for, stranger?" he rasped.

Retief got to his feet. "I think I should explain—"

A short-nosed automatic appeared in Lemuel's hand, a clashing note against his fringed buckskins. "Skip the talk. I know a fink when I see one."

"Just for a change, I'd like to finish a sentence," Retief said. "And I suggest you put your courage back in your pocket before it bites you."

"You talk too damned fancy to suit me."

"You're wrong. I talk to suit me. Now, for the last time: put it away."

Lemuel stared at Retief. "You givin' me orders . . . ?"

Retief's left fist shot out and smacked Lemuel's face dead center. The raw-boned settler stumbled back, blood starting from his nose. The pistol fired into the dirt as he dropped it. He caught himself, jumped for Retief . . . and met a straight right that snapped him onto his back—out cold.

"Wow!" said Potter. "The stranger took Lem . . . in two punches . . ."

"One," said Swazey. "That first one was just a love tap."

Bert froze. "Quiet boys," he whispered. In the sudden silence a night lizard called. Retief strained, heard nothing. He narrowed his eyes, peering past the fire.

With a swift lunge he seized up the bucket of drinking water, dashed it over the fire, and threw himself flat. He heard the others hit the dirt a split second after him.

"You move fast for a city man," breathed Swazey beside him. "You see pretty good too. We'll split and take 'em from two sides. You and Bert from the left, me and Potter from the right."

"No," said Retief. "You wait here. I'm going out alone."

"What's the idea . . . ?"

"Later. Sit tight and keep your eyes open." Retief took a bearing on a treetop faintly visible against the sky and started forward.

Five minutes' cautious progress brought Retief to a slight rise of ground. With infinite caution he raised himself and risked a glance over an outcropping of rock. The stunted trees ended just ahead. Beyond, he could make out the dim contour of rolling desert: Flap-jack country. He got to his feet, clambered over the stone, still hot after a day of tropical heat, and moved forward twenty yards. Around him he saw nothing but drifted sand, palely visible in the starlight, and the occasional shadow of jutting shale slabs. Behind him the jungle was still. He sat down on the ground to wait.

It was ten minutes before a movement caught his eye; something had separated itself from a dark mass of stone, and glided across a few yards of open ground to another shelter. Retief watched. Minutes passed. The shape moved again, slipped into a shadow ten feet distant. Retief felt the butt of the power pistol with his elbow. His guess had better be right. . . .

There was a sudden rasp, like leather against concrete, and a flurry of sand as the Flap-jack charged. Retief rolled aside, then lunged, throwing his weight on the flopping Flap-jack—a yard square, three inches thick at the center, and all muscle. The ray-like creature heaved up, curled backward, its edge rippling, to stand on the flattened rim of its encircling sphincter. It scrabbled with its prehensile fringe-tentacles for a grip on

Retief's shoulders. Retief wrapped his arms around
the creature and struggled to his feet. The thing
was heavy, a hundred pounds at least; fighting as
it was, it seemed more like five hundred.

The Flap-jack reversed its tactics, becoming limp.
Retief grabbed and felt a thumb slip into an orifice.

The creature went wild. Retief hung on, dug
the thumb in deeper.

"Sorry, fellow," he muttered between his clenched
teeth. "Eye-gouging isn't gentlemanly, but it's
effective. . . ."

The Flap-jack fell still; only its fringes rippling
slowly. Retief relaxed the pressure of his thumb.
The creature gave a tentative jerk; the thumb dug
in. The Flap-jack went limp again, waiting.

"Now that we understand each other," said Retief,
"lead me to your headquarters."

Twenty minutes' walk into the desert brought
Retief to a low rampart of thorn branches: the
Flap-jacks' outer defensive line against Terry for-
ays. It would be as good a place as any to wait for
the next move by the Flap-jacks. He sat down,
eased the weight of his captive off his back, keeping a firm thumb in place. If his analysis of the
situation was correct, a Flap-jack picket should be
along before too long. . . .

A penetrating beam of red light struck Retief in
the face, then blinked off. He got to his feet. The
captive Flap-jack rippled its fringe in an agitated
way. Retief tensed his thumb.

"Sit tight," he said. "Don't try to do anything
hasty. . . ."

His remarks were falling on deaf ears—or no ears
at all—but the thumb spoke as loudly as words.

There was a slither of sand, then another. Retief became aware of a ring of presences drawing closer.

Retief tightened his grip on the creature. He could see a dark shape now, looming up almost to his own six-three. It appeared that the Flap-jacks came in all sizes.

A low rumble sounded, like a deep-throated growl. It strummed on, then faded out. Retief cocked his head, frowning.

"Try it two octaves higher," he said.

"Awwrrp! Sorry. Is that better?" a clear voice came from the darkness.

"That's fine," Retief said. "I'm here to arrange an exchange of prisoners."

"Prisoners? But we have no prisoners."

"Sure you have. Me. Is it a deal?"

"Ah, yes, of course. Quite equitable. What guarantees do you require?"

"The word of a gentleman is sufficient." Retief released his captive. It flopped once and disappeared into the darkness.

"If you'd care to accompany me to our headquarters," the voice said, "we can discuss our mutual concerns in comfort."

"Delighted."

Red lights blinked briefly. Retief, glimpsing a gap in the thorny barrier, stepped through it. He followed dim shapes across warm sand to a low cave-like entry, faintly lit with a reddish glow.

"I must apologize for the awkward design of our comfort-dome," said the voice. "Had we known we would be honored by a visit."

"Think nothing of it," Retief said. "We diplomats are trained to crawl."

Inside, with knees bent and head ducked under

the five-foot ceiling, Retief looked around at the walls of pink-toned nacre, a floor like burgundy-colored glass spread with silken rugs, and a low table of polished red granite set out with silver dishes and rose-crystal drinking tubes.

"Let me congratulate you," the voice said. Retief turned. An immense Flap-jack, hung with crimson trappings, rippled at his side. The voice issued from a disk strapped to its back. "Your skirmish-forms fight well. I think we will find in each other worthy adversaries."

"Thanks. I'm sure the test would be interesting, but I'm hoping we can avoid it."

"Avoid it?" Retief heard a low humming coming from the speaker in the silence. "Well, let us dine," the mighty Flap-jack said at last, "we can resolve these matters later. I am called Hoshick of the Mosaic of the Two Dawns."

"I'm Retief." Hoshick waited expectantly. ". . . of the Mountain of Red Tape," Retief added.

"Take your place, Retief," said Hoshick. "I hope you won't find our rude couches uncomfortable." Two other large Flap-jacks came into the room and communed silently with Hoshick. "Pray forgive our lack of translating devices," he said to Retief. "Permit me to introduce my colleagues."

A small Flap-jack rippled into the chamber bearing on its back a silver tray, laden with aromatic food. The waiter served the diners and filled the drinking tubes with yellow wine.

"I trust you'll find these dishes palatable," Hoshick said. "Our metabolisms are much alike, I believe." Retief tried the food; it had a delicious nut-like flavor. The wine was indistinguishable from Chateau d'Yquem.

"It was an unexpected pleasure to encounter your party here," Hoshick said. "I confess at first we took you for an indigenous earth-grubbing form, but we were soon disabused of that notion." He raised a tube, manipulating it deftly with his fringe tentacles. Retief returned the salute and drank.

"Of course," Hoshick continued, "as soon as we realized that you were sportsmen like ourselves, we attempted to make amends by providing a bit of activity for you. We've ordered out our heavier equipment and a few trained skirmishers and soon we'll be able to give you an adequate show, or so I hope."

"Additional skirmishers?" said Retief. "How many, if you don't mind my asking?"

"For the moment, perhaps only a few hundred. Thereafter . . . well, I'm sure we can arrange that between us. Personally I would prefer a contest of limited scope—no nuclear or radiation-effect weapons. Such a bore, screening the spawn for deviations. Though I confess we've come upon some remarkably useful sports: the ranger-form such as you made captive, for example. Simple-minded, of course, but a fantastically keen tracker."

"Oh, by all means," Retief said. "No atomics. As you pointed out, spawn-sorting is a nuisance, and then too, it's wasteful of troops."

"Ah, well, they are after all expendable. But we agree, no atomics. Have you tried the ground-gwack eggs? Rather a specialty of my Mosaic . . ."

"Delicious," said Retief. "I wonder if you've considered eliminating weapons altogether?"

A scratchy sound issued from the disk. "Pardon my laughter," Hoshick said, "but surely you jest?"

"As a matter of fact," said Retief, "we ourselves try to avoid the use of weapons."

"I seem to recall that our first contact of skirmish-forms involved the use of a weapon by one of your units."

"My apologies," said Retief. "The—ah—skirmish-form failed to recognize that he was dealing with a sportsman."

"Still, now that we have commenced so merrily with weapons . . ." Hoshick signaled and the servant refilled the drinking tubes.

"There is an aspect I haven't yet mentioned," Retief went on. "I hope you won't take this personally, but the fact is, our skirmish-forms think of weapons as something one employs only in dealing with certain specific life-forms."

"Oh? Curious. What forms are those?"

"Vermin. Deadly antagonists, but lacking in caste. I don't want our skirmish-forms thinking of such worthy adversaries as yourself as vermin."

"Dear me! I hadn't realized, of course. Most considerate of you to point it out." Hoshick clucked in dismay. "I see that skirmish-forms are much the same among you as with us: lacking in perception." He laughed scratchily.

"Which brings us to the crux of the matter," Retief said. "You see, we're up against a serious problem with regard to skirmish-forms: a low birth rate. Therefore we've reluctantly taken to substitutes for the mass actions so dear to the heart of the sportsman. We've attempted to put an end to these contests altogether . . ."

Hoshick coughed explosively, sending a spray of wine into the air. "What are you saying?" he gasped.

"Are you proposing that Hoshick of the Mosaic of the Two Dawns abandon honor?"

"Sir!" said Retief sternly. "You forget yourself. I, Retief of the Red Tape, merely make an alternate proposal more in keeping with the newest sporting principles."

"New?" cried Hoshick. "My dear Retief, what a pleasant surprise! I'm enthralled with novel modes. One gets so out of touch. Do elaborate."

"It's quite simple, really. Each side selects a representative and the two individuals settle the issue between them."

"I . . . um . . . I'm afraid I don't understand. What possible significance could one attach to the activities of a couple of random skirmish-forms?"

"I haven't made myself clear," Retief said. He took a sip of wine. "We don't involve the skirmish-forms at all; that's quite passé."

"You don't mean . . . ?"

"That's right. You and me."

Outside the starlit sand Retief tossed aside the power pistol and followed it with the leather shirt Swazey had lent him. By the faint light he could just make out the towering figure of the Flap-jack rearing up before him, his trappings gone. A silent rank of Flap-jack retainers were grouped behind him.

"I fear I must lay aside the translator now, Retief," said Hoshick. He sighed and rippled his fringe tentacles. "My spawn-fellows will never credit this. Such a curious turn fashion has taken. How much more pleasant it is to observe the action from a distance."

"I suggest we use Tennessee rules," said Retief.

"They're very liberal: biting, gouging, stomping, kneeling, and, of course, choking, as well as the usual punching, shoving, and kicking."

"Hmmm. These gambits seem geared to forms employing rigid endo-skeletons; I fear I shall be at a disadvantage."

"Of course," Retief said, "if you'd prefer a more plebeian type of contest . . ."

"By no means. But perhaps we could rule out tentacle-twisting, just to even the balance."

"Very well. Shall we begin?"

With a rush Hoshick threw himself at Retief, who ducked, whirled, and leaped on the Flap-jack's back—and felt himself flipped clear by a mighty ripple of the alien's slab-like body. Retief rolled aside as Hoshick turned on him, jumped to his feet, and threw a punch to Hoshick's mid-section. The alien whipped his left fringe around in an arc that connected with Retief's jaw, spinning onto his back. Hoshick's weight struck Retief like a dumptruck-load of concrete. Retief twisted, trying to roll. The flat body of the creature blanketed him. He worked an arm free and drummed blows on the leathery back. Hoshick nestled closer.

Retief's air was running out. He heaved up against the smothering weight; nothing budged. He was wasting his strength.

He remembered the ranger-form he had captured. The sensitive orifice had been placed ventrally, in what would be the thoracic area. . . .

He groped, feeling tough hide set with horny granules. He would be missing skin tomorrow—if there was a tomorrow. His thumb found the orifice, and he probed.

The Flap-jack recoiled. Retief held fast, probed

deeper, groping with the other hand. If the creature were bilaterally symmetrical there would be a set of ready-made handholds. . . .

There were. Retief dug in and the Flap-jack writhed and pulled away. Retief held on, scrambled to his feet, threw his weight against Hoshick, and fell on top of him, still gouging. Hoshick rippled his fringe wildly, flopped in distress, then went limp. Retief relaxed, released his hold, and got to his feet, breathing hard. Hoshick humped himself over onto his ventral side, lifted, and moved gingerly over to the sidelines. His retainers came forward, assisted him into his trappings, and strapped on the translator. He sighed heavily, adjusting the volume.

"There is much to be said for the old system," he said. "What a burden one's sportsmanship places on one at times."

"Great fun, wasn't it?" said Retief. "Now, I know you'll be eager to continue. If you'll just wait while I run back and fetch some of our gouger-forms—"

"May hide-ticks devour the gouger-forms!" Hoshick bellowed. "You've given me such a sprong-ache as I'll remember each spawning-time for a year."

"Speaking of hide-ticks," said Retief, "we've developed a biter-form—"

"Enough!" Hoshick roared so loudly that the translator bounced on his hide. "Suddenly I yearn for the crowded yellow sands of Jaq. I had hoped . . ." He broke off, drawing a rasping breath. "I had hoped, Retief," he said, speaking sadly now, "to find a new land here where I might plan my own Mosaic, till these alien sands and bring forth such a crop of paradise-lichen as should glut the markets of a hundred worlds. But my spirit is not equal to the prospect of biter-forms and gouger-forms without end. I am shamed before you."

"To tell you the truth, I'm old-fashioned myself," said Retief. "I'd rather watch the action from a distance too."

"But surely your spawn-fellows would never condone such an attitude."

"My spawn-fellows aren't here. And besides, didn't I mention it? No one who's really in the know would think of engaging in competition by mere combat if there were any other way. Now, you mentioned tilling the sand, raising lichens—"

"That on which we dined," said Hoshick, "and from which the wine is made."

"The big trend in fashionable diplomacy today is farming competition. Now, if you'd like to take these deserts and raise lichen, we'll promise to stick to the oases and raise vegetables."

Hoshick curled his back in attention. "Retief, you're quite serious? You would leave all the fair sand hills to us?"

"The whole works, Hoshick. I'll take the oases."

Hoshick rippled his fringes ecstatically. "Once again you have outdone me, Retief," he cried, "this time, in generosity."

"We'll talk over the details later. I'm sure we can establish a set of rules that will satisfy all parties. Now I've got to get back. I think some of the gouger-forms are waiting to see me."

It was nearly dawn when Retief gave the whistled signal he had agreed on with Potter, then rose and walked into the camp circle. Swazey stood up.

"There you are," he said. "We been wonderin' whether to go out after you."

Lemuel came forward, one eye black to the cheekbone. He held out a raw-boned hand. "Sorry I jumped you, stranger. Tell you the truth, I thought you was some kind of stool-pigeon from the CDT."

Bert came up behind Lemuel. "How do you know he ain't, Lemuel?" he said. "Maybe he—"

Lemuel floored Bert with a backward sweep of his arm. "Next cotton-picker says some embassy Johnny can cool me gets worse'n that."

"Tell me," said Retief. "How are you boys fixed for wine?"

"Wine? Mister, we been livin' on stump water for a year now. 'Dobe's fatal to the kind of bacteria it takes to ferment liquor."

"Try this." Retief handed over a squat jug. Swazey drew the cork, sniffed, drank, and passed it to Lemuel.

"Mister, where'd you get that?"

"The Flap-jack make it. Here's another question for you: would you concede a share in this planet to the Flap-jacks in return for a peace guarantee?"

At the end of a half hour of heated debate Lemuel turned to Retief. "We'll make any reasonable deal," he said. "I guess they got as much right here as we have. I think we'd agree to a fifty-fifty split. That'd give about a hundred and fifty oases to each side."

"What would you say to keeping all the oases and giving them the desert?"

Lemuel reached for the wine jug, his eyes on Retief. "Keep talkin', mister," he said. "I think you got yourself a deal."

*   *   *

Consul Passwyn glanced up as Retief entered the office.

"Sit down, Retief," he said absently. "I thought you were over on Pueblo, or Mud-flat, or whatever they call that desert."

"I'm back."

Passwyn eyed him sharply. "Well, well, what is it you need, man? Speak up. Don't expect me to request any military assistance."

Retief passed a bundle of documents across the desk. "Here's the Treaty. And a Mutual Assistance Pact and a Trade Agreement."

"Eh?" Passwyn picked up the papers and riffled through them. He leaned back in his chair, beaming.

"Well, Retief, expeditiously handled." He stopped and blinked at the Vice-Consul. "You seem to have a bruise on your jaw. I hope you've been conducting yourself as befits a member of the Consulate staff."

"I attended a sporting event. One of the players got a little excited."

"Well . . . it's one of the hazards of the profession. One must pretend an interest in such matters." Passwyn rose and extended a hand. "You've done well, my boy. Let this teach you the value of following instructions to the letter."

Outside, by the hall incinerator drop, Retief paused long enough to take from his briefcase a large buff envelope, still sealed, and drop it in the slot.

Cultural
Exchange

. . . Highly effective ancillary programs, developed early in Corps history, played a vital role in promoting harmony among the peace-loving peoples of the Galactic community. The notable success of Assistant Attaché (later Ambassador) Magnan in the cosmopolitization of reactionary elements in the Nicodeman Cluster was achieved through the agency of these enlightened programs. . . .

Vol. III, reel 71 482 A. E. (AD 2943)

First Secretary Magnan took his green-lined cape and orange-feathered beret from the clothes tree. "I'm off now, Retief," he said. "I hope you'll manage the administrative routine during my absence without any unfortunate incidents."

"That seems a modest enough hope," said Second Secretary Retief. "I'll try to live up to it."

"I don't appreciate frivolity with reference to this Division," Magnan said testily. "When I first came here, the Manpower Utilization Directorate, Division of Libraries and Education was a shambles. I fancy I've made MUDDLE what it is today. Frankly, I question the wisdom of placing you in charge of such a sensitive desk, even for two weeks; but remember, yours is a purely rubber-stamp function."

"In that case, let's leave it to Miss Furkle, and I'll take a couple of weeks off myself. With her poundage, she could bring plenty of pressure to bear."

"I assume you jest, Retief," Magnan said sadly. "I should expect even you to appreciate that Bogan participation in the Exchange Program may be the first step toward sublimation of their aggressions into more cultivated channels."

"I see they're sending two thousand students to d'Land," Retief said, glancing at the Memo for Record. "That's a sizable sublimation."

Magnan nodded. "The Bogans have launched no less than four military campaigns in the last two decades. They're known as the Hoodlums of the Nicodeman Cluster. Now, perhaps, we shall see them breaking that precedent and entering into the cultural life of the Galaxy."

"Breaking and entering," Retief said. "You may have something there. But I'm wondering what they'll study on d'Land. That's an industrial world of the poor-but-honest variety."

"Academic details are the affair of the students and their professors," Magnan said. "Our function is merely to bring them together. See that you don't antagonize the Bogan representative. This will be an excellent opportunity for you to practice your diplomatic restraint—not your strong point, I'm sure you'll agree—"

A buzzer sounded. Retief punched a button. "What is it, Miss Furkle?"

"That—bucolic person from Lovenbroy is here again." On the small desk screen, Miss Furkle's meaty features were compressed in disapproval.

"This fellow's a confounded pest; I'll leave him to you, Retief," Magnan said. "Tell him something; get rid of him. And remember: here at Corps HQ, all eyes are upon you."

"If I'd thought of that, I'd have worn my other suit," Retief said.

Magnan snorted and passed from view. Retief punched Miss Furkle's button.

"Send the bucolic person in."

A tall broad man with bronze skin and grey hair, wearing tight trousers of heavy cloth, a loose shirt open at the neck, and a short jacket, stepped into the room; a bundle under his arm. He paused at sight of Retief, looked him over momentarily, then advanced and held out his hand. Retief took it. For a moment the two big men stood, face to face. The newcomer's jaw muscles knotted. Then he winced. Retief dropped his hand, motioned to a chair.

"That's nice knuckle work, mister," the stranger said, massaging his hand. "First time anybody ever did that to me. My fault, though, I started it, I guess." He grinned and sat down.

"What can I do for you?" the Second Secretary said. "My name's Retief. I'm taking Mr. Magnan's place for a couple of weeks."

"You work for this culture bunch, do you? Funny, I thought they were all ribbon-counter boys. Never mind. I'm Hank Arapoulous. I'm a farmer. What I wanted to see you about was—" He shifted in his chair. "Well, out on Lovenbroy we've got a serious problem. The wine crop is just about ready. We start picking in another two, three months. Now I don't know if you're familiar with the Bacchus vines we grow?"

"No," Retief said. "Have a cigar?" He pushed a box across the desk. Arapoulous took one. "Bacchus vines are an unusual crop," he said, puffing life into the cigar. "Only mature every twelve years.

In between, the vines don't need a lot of attention; our time's mostly our own. We like to farm, though. Spend a lot of time developing new forms. Apples the size of a melon—and sweet."

"Sounds very pleasant," Retief said. "Where does the Libraries and Education Division come in?"

Arapoulous leaned forward. "We go in pretty heavy for the arts. Folks can't spend all their time hybridizing plants. We've turned all the land area we've got into parks and farms; course, we left some sizable forest areas for hunting and such. Lovenbroy's a nice place, Mr. Retief."

"It sounds like it, Mr. Arapoulous. Just what—"

"Call me Hank. We've got long seasons back home. Five of 'em. Our year's about eighteen Terry months. Cold as hell in winter—eccentric orbit, you know. Blue-black sky, stars visible all day. We do mostly painting and sculpture in the winter. Then Spring—still plenty cold. Lots of skiing, bob-sledding, ice skating—and it's the season for woodworkers. Our furniture—"

"I've seen some of your furniture, I believe," said Retief. "Beautiful work."

Arapoulous nodded. "All local timbers, too. Lots of metals in our soil; those sulphates give the woods some color, I'll tell you. Then comes the Monsoon. Rain—it comes down in sheets—but the sun's gettin' closer; shines all the time. Ever seen it pouring rain in the sunshine? That's the music-writing season. Then summer. Summer's hot. We stay inside in the daytime, and have beach parties all night. Lots of beach on Lovenbroy, we're mostly islands. That's the drama and symphony time. The theatres are set up on the sand, or anchored on barges off-shore. You have the music and the surf and the bonfires and stars—we're close to the center of a globular cluster, you know. . . ."

"You say it's time now for the wine crop?"

"That's right. Autumn's our harvest season. Most years we have just the ordinary crops; fruit, grain, that kind of thing. Getting it in doesn't take long. We spend most of the time on architecture, getting new places ready for the winter, or remodeling the older ones. We spend a lot of time in our houses; we like to have them comfortable. But this year's different. This is Wine Year."

Arapoulous puffed on his cigar and looked worriedly at Retief. "Our wine crop is our big money crop," he said. "We make enough to keep us going. But this year . . ."

"The crop isn't panning out?"

"Oh, the crop's fine; one of the best I can remember. Course, I'm only twenty-eight; I can't remember but two other harvests. The problem's not the crop. . . ."

"Have you lost your markets? That sounds like a matter for the Commercial—"

"Lost our markets? Mister, nobody that ever tasted our wines ever settled for anything else!"

"It sounds like I've been missing something," said Retief. "I'll have to try them some time."

Arapoulous put his bundle on the desk, pulled off the wrappings. "No time like the present," he said.

Retief looked at the two squat bottles, one green, one amber, both dusty, with faded labels, and blackened corks secured by wire.

"Drinking on duty is frowned on in the Corps, Mr. Arapoulous," he said.

"This isn't drinking, it's just wine." Arapoulous

pulled the wire retainer loose and thumbed the cork. It rose slowly, then popped in the air. Arapoulous caught it. Aromatic fumes wafted from the bottle. "Besides, my feelings would be hurt if you didn't join me." He winked.

Retief took two thin-walled glasses from a table beside the desk. "Come to think of it, we also have to be careful about violating quaint native customs." Arapoulous filled the glasses. Retief picked one up, sniffed the deep rust colored fluid, tasted it, then took a healthy swallow. He looked at Arapoulous thoughtfully.

"Hmmm, it tastes like salted pecans, with an undercurrent of crusted port."

"Don't try to describe it, Mr. Retief," Arapoulous said. He took a mouthful of wine, swished it around his teeth, and swallowed. "It's Bacchus wine, that's all." He pushed the second bottle toward Retief. "The custom back home is to alternate red wine and black."

Retief put aside his cigar, pulled the wires loose, nudged the cork, and caught it as it popped up.

"Bad luck if you miss the cork," Arapoulous said, nodding. "You probably never heard about the trouble we had on Lovenbroy a few years back?"

"Can't say that I did, Hank." Retief poured the black wine into the two fresh glasses. "Here's to the harvest."

"We've got plenty of minerals on Lovenbroy," Arapoulous said, swallowing wine. "But we don't plan to wreck the landscape mining 'em. We like to farm. About ten years back some neighbors of ours landed a force. They figured they knew better what to do with our minerals than we did.

Wanted to strip-mine, smelt ore. We convinced 'em otherwise. But it took a year, and we lost a lot of men."

"That's too bad," Retief said. "I'd say this one tastes more like roast beef and popcorn over a Riesling base."

"It put us in a bad spot," Arapoulous went on. "We had to borrow money from a world called Croanie, mortgaged our crops; we had to start exporting art work too. Plenty of buyers, but it's not the same when you're doing it for strangers."

"What's the problem?" Retief said, "Croanie about to foreclose?"

"The loan's due. The wine crop would put us in the clear; but we need harvest hands. Picking Bacchus grapes isn't a job you can turn over to machinery—and we wouldn't if we could. Vintage season is the high point of living on Lovenbroy. Everybody joins in. First, there's the picking in the fields. Miles and miles of vineyards covering the mountain sides, crowding the river banks, with gardens here and there. Big vines, eight feet high, loaded with fruit, and deep grass growing between. The wine-carriers keep on the run, bringing wine to the pickers. There's prizes for the biggest day's output, bets on who can fill the most baskets in an hour. The sun's high and bright, and it's just cool enough to give you plenty of energy. Come night-fall the tables are set up in the garden plots, and the feast is laid on: roast turkeys, beef, hams, all kinds of fowl. Big salads and plenty of fruit and fresh-baked bread . . . and wine, plenty of wine. The cooking's done by a different crew each night in each garden, and there's prizes for the best crews.

"Then the wine-making. We still tramp out the vintage. That's mostly for the young folks—but anybody's welcome. That's when things start to get loosened up. Matter of fact, pretty near half our young-uns are born about nine months after a vintage. All bets are off then. It keeps a fellow on his toes though; ever tried to hold onto a gal wearin' nothing but a layer of grape juice?"

"Never did," Retief said. "You say most of the children are born after a vintage. That would make them only twelve years old by the time—"

"Oh, that's Lovenbroy years; they'd be eighteen, Terry reckoning."

"I was thinking you looked a little mature for twenty-eight," Retief said.

"Forty-two, Terry years," Arapoulous said. "But this year—it looks bad. "We've got a bumper crop— and we're short-handed. If we don't get a big vintage, Croanie steps in; lord knows what they'll do to the land.

"What we figured was, maybe you Culture boys could help us out; a loan to see us through the vintage, enough to hire extra hands. Then we'd repay it in sculpture, painting, furniture—"

"Sorry, Hank. All we do here is work out itineraries for traveling side-shows, that kind of thing. Now if you needed a troop of Groaci nose-flute players—"

"Can they pick grapes?"

"Nope—anyway they can't stand the daylight. Have you talked this over with the Labor office?"

"Sure did. They said they'd fix us up with all the electronics specialists and computer programmers we wanted—but no field hands. Said it was what they classified as menial drudgery; you'd have thought I was trying to buy slaves."

The buzzer sounded. Miss Furkle appeared on the desk screen.

"You're due at the Inter-Group Council in five minutes," she said. "Then afterwards, there are the Bogan students to meet."

"Thanks," Retief finished his glass and stood. "I have to run, Hank," he said. "Let me think this over. Maybe I can come up with something. Check with me day after tomorrow. And you'd better leave the bottles here. Cultural exhibits, you know."

As the council meeting broke up, Retief caught the eye of a colleague across the table.

"Mr. Whaffle, you mentioned a shipment going to a place called Croanie. What are they getting?"

Whaffle blinked. "You're the fellow who's filling in for Magnan, over at MUDDLE," he said. "Properly speaking, equipment grants are the sole concern of the Motorized Equipment Depot, Division of Loans and Exchanges." He pursed his lips. "However, I suppose there's no harm in my telling you. They'll be receiving heavy mining equipment."

"Drill rigs, that sort of thing?"

"Strip mining gear." Whaffle took a slip of paper from a breast pocket and blinked at it. "Bolo Model WV/1 tractors, to be specific. Why MUDDLE's interest in MEDDLE's activities?"

"Forgive my curiosity, Mr. Whaffle. It's just that Croanie cropped up earlier today; seems she holds a mortgage on some vineyards over on—"

"That's not MEDDLE's affair, sir," Whaffle cut

in. "I have sufficient problems as Chief of MED-DLE without probing into MUDDLE's business."

"Speaking of tractors," another man put in, "we over at the Special Committee for Rehabilitation and Overhaul of Underdeveloped Nations' General Economies have been trying for months to get a request for mining equipment for d'Land through MEDDLE—"

"SCROUNGE was late on the scene," Whaffle said. "First come, first served, that's our policy at MEDDLE. Good day, gentlemen." He strode off, a briefcase under his arm.

"That's the trouble with peaceful worlds," the SCROUNGE committeeman said. "Boge is a trouble-maker, so every agency in the Corps is out to pacify her, while my chance to make a record—that is, assist peace-loving d'Land, comes to nought."

"What kind of university do they have on d'Land?" asked Retief. "We're sending them two thousand exchange students. It must be quite an institution—"

"University? D'Land has one under-endowed technical college."

"Will all the exchange students be studying at the Technical College?"

"Two thousand students? Hah! Two hundred students would overtax the facilities of the college!"

"I wonder if the Bogans know that?"

"The Bogans? Why, most of d'Land's difficulties are due to the unwise trade agreement she entered into with Boge. Two thousand students indeed." He snorted and walked away.

Retief stopped by the office to pick up his short violet cape, then rode the elevator to the roof of the 230-story Corps HQ building and hailed a cab to the port. The Bogan students had arrived early. Retief saw them lined up on the ramp waiting to go through customs. It would be half an hour before they were cleared through. He turned into the bar and ordered a beer. A tall young fellow on the next stool raised his glass.

"Happy days," he said.

"And nights to match."

"You said it." He gulped half his beer. "My name's Karsh. Mr. Karsh. Yep, Mr. Karsh. Boy, this is a drag, sitting around this place waiting."

"You meeting somebody?"

"Yeah. Bunch of babies. Kids. How they expect— Never mind. Have one on me."

"Thanks. You a scoutmaster?"

"I'll tell you what I am; I'm a cradle-robber. You know," he turned to Retief, "not one of those kids is over eighteen." He hiccupped. "Students, you know. Never saw a student with a beard, did you?"

"Lots of times. You're meeting the students, are you?"

The young fellow blinked at Retief. "Oh, you know about it, huh?"

"I represent MUDDLE."

Karsh finished his beer and ordered another. "I came on ahead: sort of an advance guard for the kids. I trained 'em myself. Treated it like a game, but they can handle a CSU. Don't know how they'll act under pressure. If I had my old platoon—"

He looked at his beer glass, then pushed it back. "Had enough," he said. "So long, friend. Or are you coming along?"

Retief nodded. "Might as well."

At the exit to the Customs enclosure, Retief watched as the first of the Bogan students came through, caught sight of Karsh, and snapped to attention.

"Drop that, mister," Karsh snapped. "Is that any way for a student to act?"

The youth, a round-faced lad with broad shoulders, grinned.

"Guess not," he said. "Say, uh, Mr. Karsh, are we gonna get to go to town. Us fellas were thinkin'—"

"You were, hah? You act like a bunch of school kids—I mean . . . No! Now line up!"

"We have quarters ready for the students," Retief said. "If you'd like to bring them around to the west side, I have a couple of copters laid on."

"Thanks," said Karsh. "They'll stay here until take-off time. Can't have the little darlings wandering around loose. Might get ideas about going over the hill." He hiccupped. "I mean, they might play hookey."

"We've scheduled your re-embarkation for noon tomorrow. That's a long wait. MUDDLE's arranged theatre tickets and a dinner."

"Sorry," Karsh said. "As soon as the baggage gets here, we're off." He hiccupped again. "Can't travel without our baggage, y'know."

"Suit yourself," Retief said. "Where's the baggage now?"

"Coming in aboard a Croanie lighter."

"Maybe you'd like to arrange for a meal for the students here?"

"Sure," Karsh said. "That's a good idea. Why don't you join us?" Karsh winked. "And bring a few beers."

"Not this time," Retief said. He watched the students, still emerging from Customs. "They seem to be all boys," he commented. "No female students?"

"Maybe later," Karsh said, "after we see how the first bunch is received."

Back at the MUDDLE office, Retief buzzed Miss Furkle.

"Do you know the name of the institution these Bogan students are bound for?"

"Why, the university at d'Land, of course."

"Would that be the Technical College?"

Miss Furkle's mouth puckered. "I'm sure I've never pried into these details—"

"Where does doing your job stop and prying begin, Miss Furkle?" Retief said. "Personally, I'm curious as to just what it is these students are travelling so far to study—at Corps expense."

"Mr. Magnan never—"

"For the present, Miss Furkle, Mr. Magnan is vacationing. That leaves me with the question of two thousand young male students headed for a world with no classrooms for them . . . a world in need of tractors. But the tractors are on their way to Croanie, a world under obligations to Boge. And Croanie holds a mortgage on the best grape acreage on Lovenbroy."

"Well!" Miss Furkle snapped, her small eyes glaring under unplucked brows. "I hope you're not questioning Mr. Magnan's wisdom!"

"About Mr. Magnan's wisdom there can be no doubts," Retief said. "But never mind. I'd like you to look up an item for me. How many tractors will Croanie be getting under the MEDDLE program?"

"Why, that's entirely MEDDLE business," Miss Furkle said. "Mr. Magnan always—"

"I'm sure he did. Let me know about the tractors as soon as you can."

Miss Furkle sniffed and disappeared from the screen. Retief left the office, descended forty-one stories, and followed a corridor to the Corps Library. In the stacks he thumbed through catalogs and pored over indices.

"Can I help you?" someone chirped. A tiny librarian stood at his elbow.

"Thank you, Ma'am," Retief said. "I'm looking for information on a mining rig: a Bolo model WV tractor."

"You won't find it in the industrial section," the librarian said. "Come along." Retief followed her along the stacks to a well-lit section lettered ARMAMENTS. She took a tape from the shelf, plugged it into the viewer, flipped through, and stopped at a picture of a squat armored vehicle.

"That's the model WV," she said. "It's what is known as a Continental Siege Unit. It carries four men, with a half-megaton/second firepower—"

"There must be an error somewhere," Retief said. "The Bolo model I want is a tractor, model WV M-1—"

"Oh, the modification was the addition of a blade for demolition work. That must be what confused you."

"Probably—among other things. Thank you."

Miss Furkle was waiting at the office. "I have the information you wanted," she said. "I've had it for over ten minutes. I was under the impression you needed it urgently, and I went to great lengths—"

"Sure," Retief said. "Shoot. How many tractors?"

"Five hundred."

"Are you sure?"

Miss Furkle's chins quivered. "Well! If you feel I'm incompetent."

"Just questioning the possibility of a mistake, Miss Furkle. Five hundred tractors is a lot of equipment."

"Was there anything further?" Miss Furkle inquired frigidly.

"I sincerely hope not," Retief said.

Leaning back in Magnan's padded chair with its power swivel and hip-u-matic contour, Retief leafed through a folder labelled "CERP 7-602-Ba; CROANIE (general)." He paused at a page headed INDUSTRY. Still reading, he opened the desk drawer, took out the two bottles of Bacchus wine and two glasses. He poured an inch of wine into each, then sipped the black wine meditatively. It would be a pity, he reflected, if anything should interfere with the production of such vintages. . . .

Half an hour later he laid the folder aside, keyed the phone, and put through a call to the Croanie Legation, asking for the Commercial attaché.

"Retief here, Corps HQ," he said airily. "About the MEDDLE shipment, the tractors. I'm wondering if there's been a slip-up. My records show we're shipping five hundred units."

"That's correct. Five hundred."

Retief waited.

"Ah . . . are you there, Mr. Retief?"

"I'm still here. And I'm wondering about the five hundred tractors."

"It's perfectly in order; I thought it was all settled. Mr. Whaffle—"

"One unit would require a good-sized plant to handle its output," Retief said. "Now Croanie subsists on her fisheries. She has perhaps half-a-dozen pint-sized processing plants. Maybe, in a bind, they could handle the ore ten WV's could scrape up . . . if Croanie had any ore. By the way, isn't a WV a poor choice as a mining outfit? I should think—"

"See here, Retief, why all this interest in a few surplus tractors? And in any event, what business is it of yours how we plan to use the equipment? That's an internal affair of my government. Mr. Whaffle—"

"I'm not Mr. Whaffle. What are you going to do with the other four hundred and ninety tractors?"

"I understood the grant was to be with no strings attached!"

"I know it's bad manners to ask questions. It's an old diplomatic tradition that any time you can get anybody to accept anything as a gift, you've scored points in the game. But if Croanie has some scheme cooking—"

"Nothing like that, Retief! It's a mere business transaction."

"What kind of business do you do with a Bolo WV? With or without a blade attached, it's what's known as a continental siege unit—"

"Great Heavens, Retief! Don't jump to conclusions! Would you have us branded as warmongers? Frankly—is this a closed line?"

"Certainly. You may speak freely."

"The tractors are for trans-shipment. We've gotten ourselves into a difficult situation in our balance of payments. This is an accommodation to a group with which we have strong business ties."

"I understand you hold a mortgage on the best land on Lovenbroy," Retief said. "Any connection?"

"Why . . . ah . . . no. Of course not."

"Who gets the tractors eventually?"

"Retief, this is unwarranted interference—"

"Who gets them?"

"They happen to be going to Lovenbroy. But I scarcely see—"

"And who's the friend you're helping out with an unauthorized trans-shipment of grant material?"

"Why . . . ah . . . I've been working with a Mr. Gulver, a Bogan representative."

"And when will they be shipped?"

"Why, they went out a week ago. They'll be halfway there by now. But look here, Retief, this isn't what you're thinking!"

"How do you know what I'm thinking? I don't know myself." Retief rang off and buzzed the secretary.

"Miss Furkle, I'd like to be notified immediately of any new applications that might come in from the Bogan Consulate for placement of students."

"Well, it happens, by coincidence, that I have an application here now. Mr. Gulver of the Consulate brought it in."

"Is Mr. Gulver in the office? I'd like to see him."

"I'll ask him if he has time."

It was half a minute before a thick-necked red-faced man in a tight hat walked in. He wore an old-fashioned suit, a drab shirt, shiny shoes with round toes, and an ill-tempered expression.

"What is it you wish?" he barked. "I understood in my discussions with the other . . . ah . . . civilian there'd be no further need for these irritating conferences."

"I've just learned you're placing more students abroad, Mr. Gulver. How many this time?"

"Three thousand."

"And where will they be going?"

"Croanie—it's all in the application form I've handed in. Your job is to provide transportation."

"Will there be any other students embarking this season?"

"Why . . . perhaps. That's Boge's business." Gulver looked at Retief with pursed lips. "As a matter of fact, we have in mind dispatching another two thousand to Featherweight."

"Another under-populated world—and in the same cluster, I believe," Retief said. "Your people must be unusually interested in that region of space."

"If that's all you wanted to know, I'll be on my way. I have matters of importance to see to."

After Gulver left Retief called Miss Furkle in. "I'd like to have a break-out of all the student movements that have been planned under the present program," he said. "And see if you can get a summery of what MEDDLE has been shipping lately."

Miss Furkle bridled. "If Mr. Magnan were here, I'm sure he wouldn't dream of interfering in the work of other departments. I . . . overheard your conversation with the gentleman from the Croanie Legation—"

"The lists, Miss Furkle."

"I'm not accustomed," Miss Furkle said, "to intruding in matters outside our interest cluster."

"That's worse than listening in on phone conversations, eh? But never mind. I need the information, Miss Furkle."

"Loyalty to my Chief—"

"Loyalty to your pay-check should send you scuttling for the material I've asked for," Retief said. "I'm taking full responsibility. Now scat."

The buzzer sounded. Retief flipped a key. "MUDDLE, Retief speaking . . ."

Arapoulous' brown face appeared on the desk screen.

"How do, Retief. Okay if I come up?"

"Sure, Hank. I want to talk to you."

In the office, Arapoulous took a chair. "Sorry if I'm rushing you, Retief," he said. "But have you got anything for me?"

Retief waved at the wine bottles. "What do you know about Croanie?"

"Croanie? Not much of a place. Mostly ocean. All right if you like fish, I guess. We import some seafood from there. Nice prawns in monsoon time. Over a foot long."

"You on good terms with them?"

"Sure, I guess so. Course, they're pretty thick with Boge."

"So?"

"Didn't I tell you? Boge was the bunch that tried to take us over here a dozen years back. They would have made it, too, if they hadn't had a lot of bad luck. Their armor went in the drink, and without armor they're easy game."

Miss Furkle buzzed. "I have your lists," she said shortly.

"Bring them in, please."

The secretary placed the papers on the desk. Arapoulous caught her eye and grinned. She sniffed and marched from the room.

"What that gal needs is a slippery time in the grape mash," Arapoulous observed. Retief thumbed through the papers, pausing to read from time to time. He finished and looked at Arapoulous.

"How many men do you need for the harvest, Hank?" Retief inquired.

Arapoulous sniffed his wine glass.

"A hundred would help," he said. "A thousand would be better. Cheers."

"What would you say to two thousand?"

"Two thousand? Retief, you're not foolin'?"

"I hope not." He picked up the phone, called the Port Authority, and asked for the dispatch clerk.

"Hello, Jim. Say, I have a favor to ask of you. You know that contingent of Bogan students; they're travelling aboard the two CDT transports. I'm interested in the baggage that goes with the students. Has it arrived yet? Okay, I'll wait. . . ."

Jim came back to the phone. "Yeah, Retief, it's here. Just arrived. But there's a funny thing. It's not consigned to d'Land; it's ticketed clear through to Lovenbroy."

"Listen, Jim," Retief said. "I want you to go over to the warehouse and take a look at that baggage for me."

Retief waited while the dispatch clerk carried out the errand. The level in the two bottles had gone down an inch when Jim returned to the phone.

"Hey, I took a look at that baggage, Retief.

Something funny going on. Guns. 2mm needlers, Mark XII hand blasters, power pistols—"

"It's okay, Jim. Nothing to worry about. Just a mix-up. Now, Jim, I'm going to ask you to do something more for me. I'm covering for a friend; it seems he slipped up. I wouldn't want word to get out, you understand. I'll send along a written change order in the morning that will cover you officially. Meanwhile, here's what I want you to do. . . ."

Retief gave instructions, then rang off and turned to Arapoulous.

"As soon as I get off a couple of TWX's, we'd better get down to the port, Hank. I think I'd like to see the students off personally."

Karsh met Retief as he entered the Departures enclosure at the port.

"What's going on here?" he demanded. "There's some funny business with my baggage consignment; they won't let me see it. I've got a feeling it's not being loaded."

"You'd better hurry, Mr. Karsh," Retief said. "You're scheduled to blast off in less than an hour. Are the students all loaded?"

"Yes, blast you! What about the baggage? Those vessels aren't moving without it!"

"No need to get so upset about a few tooth-brushes, is there, Mr. Karsh?" Retief said blandly. "Still, if you're worried—" He turned to Arapoulous.

"Hank, why don't you walk Mr. Karsh over to the warehouse and . . . ah . . take care of him?"

"I know just how to handle it," Arapoulous said.

The dispatch clerk came up to Retief. "I caught the tractor shipment," he said. "Funny kind of mistake, but it's okay now. They're being off-loaded at d'Land. I talked to the traffic controller there; he said they weren't looking for any students."

"The labels got switched, Jim. The students go where the baggage was consigned; too bad about the mistake there, but the Armaments Office will have a man along in a little while to dispose of the guns. Keep an eye out for the real luggage; no telling where it's gotten to—"

"Here!" a hoarse voice yelled. Retief turned. A disheveled figure in a tight hat was crossing the enclosure, his arms waving.

"Hi there, Mr. Gulver," Retief called. "How's Boge's business coming along?"

"Piracy!" Gulver blurted as he came up to Retief. "You've got a hand in this, I don't doubt! Where's that Magnan fellow. . . ."

"What seems to be the problem?" Retief said.

"Hold those transports! I've just been notified that the baggage shipment has been impounded. I'll remind you, that shipment enjoys diplomatic free entry."

"Who told you it was impounded?"

"Never mind! I have my sources!"

Two tall men buttoned into grey tunics came up. "Are you Mr. Retief of CDT?" one said.

"That's right."

"What about my baggage!" Gulver cut in. "And I'm warning you, if those ships lift without—"

"These gentlemen are from the Armaments Control Commission," Retief said. "Would you like to come along and claim your baggage, Mr. Gulver?"

"From what? I . . ." Gulver turned two shades redder about the ears. "Armaments . . . ?"

"The only shipment I've held up seems to be

somebody's arsenal," Retief said. "Now, if you claim this is your baggage . . ."

"Why, impossible," Gulver said in a strained voice. "Armaments? Ridiculous. There's been an error."

At the baggage warehouse, Gulver looked glumly at the opened cases of guns. "No, of course not," he said dully. "Not my baggage. Not my baggage at all."

Arapoulous appeared, supporting the stumbling figure of Mr. Karsh.

"What—what's this?" Gulver sputtered. "Karsh? What's happened . . . ?"

"He had a little fall. He'll be okay," Arapoulous said.

"You'd better help him to the ship," Retief said. "It's ready to lift. We wouldn't want him to miss it."

"Leave him to me!" Gulver snapped, his eyes slashing at Karsh. "I'll see he's dealt with."

"I couldn't think of it," Retief said. "He's a guest of the Corps, you know. We'll see him safely aboard."

Gulver turned and signalled frantically. Three heavyset men in identical drab suits detached themselves from the wall and crossed to the group.

"Take this man," Gulver snapped, indicating Karsh, who looked at him dazedly.

"We take our hospitality seriously," Retief said. "We'll see him aboard the vessel."

Gulver opened his mouth—

"I know you feel bad about finding guns instead of school books in your luggage," Retief said, looking Gulver in the eye. "You'll be busy straightening out the details of the mix-up. You'll want to avoid further complications."

"Ah . . . yes," Gulver said.

Arapoulous went on to the passenger conveyor, then turned to wave.

"Your man—he's going too?" Gulver blurted.

"He's not our man, properly speaking," Retief said. "He lives on Lovenbroy."

"Lovenbroy?" Gulver choked. "But . . . the . . . I . . ."

"I know you said the students were bound for d'Land," Retief said. "But I guess that was just another aspect of the general confusion. The course plugged into the navigators was to Lovenbroy. You'll be glad to know they're still headed there—even without the baggage."

"Perhaps," Gulver said grimly, "perhaps they'll manage without it."

"By the way," Retief said. "There was another funny mix-up. There were some tractors—for industrial use, you'll recall. I believe you co-operated with Croanie in arranging the grant through MEDDLE. They were erroneously consigned to Lovenbroy, a purely agriculturial world. I saved you some embarrassment, I trust, Mr. Gulver, by arranging to have them off-loaded at d'Land."

"D'Land! You've put the CSU's in the hands of Boge's bitterest enemies . . . ?"

"But they're only tractors, Mr. Gulver. Peaceful devices. Isn't that correct?"

"That's . . . correct." Gulver sagged. Then he snapped erect. "Hold the ships!" he yelled. "I'm cancelling the student exchange."

His voice was drowned by the rumble as the first of the monster transports rose from the launch pit, followed a moment later by the second. Retief watched them fade out of sight, then turned to Gulver.

"They're off," he said. "Let's hope they get a liberal education."

Retief lay on his back in deep grass by a stream, eating grapes. A tall figure, appearing on the knoll above him, waved.

"Retief!" Hank Arapoulous bounded down the slope. "I heard you were here—and I've got news for you. You won the final day's picking competition. Over two hundred bushels! That's a record! Let's get on over to the garden, shall we? Sounds like the celebration's about to start."

In the flower-crowded park among the stripped vines, Retief and Arapoulous made their way to a laden table under the lanterns. A tall girl dressed in a loose white garment, with long golden hair, came up to Arapoulous.

"Delinda, this is Retief—today's winner. And he's also the fellow that got those workers for us."

Delinda smiled at Retief. "I've heard about you, Mr. Retief. We weren't sure about the boys at first; two thousand Bogans, and all confused about their baggage that went astray. But they seemed to like the picking. . . ." She smiled again.

"That's not all; our gals liked the boys," Hank said. "Even Bogans aren't so bad, minus their irons. A lot of 'em will be staying on. But how come you didn't tell me you were coming, Retief? I'd have laid on some kind of big welcome."

"I liked the welcome I got. And I didn't have much notice. Mr. Magnan was a little upset when he got back. It seems I exceeded my authority."

Arapoulous laughed. "I had a feeling you were wheelin' pretty free, Retief. I hope you didn't get into any trouble over it."

"No trouble," Retief said. "A few people were a little unhappy with me. It seems I'm not ready for important assignments at Departmental level. I was shipped off here to the boondocks to get a little more field experience."

"Delinda, look after Retief," said Arapoulous. "I'll see you later. I've got to see to the wine judging." He disappeared in the crowd.

"Congratulations on winning the day," said Delinda. "I noticed you at work. You were wonderful. I'm glad you're going to have the prize."

"Thanks. I noticed you too, flitting around in that white nightie of yours. But why weren't you picking grapes with the rest of us?"

"I had a special assignment."

"Too bad. You should have had a chance at the prize."

Delinda took Retief's hand. "I wouldn't have anyway," she said. "I'm the prize."

Aide Memoire

. . . Supplementing broad knowledge of affairs with such shrewd gambits as identification with significant local groups, and the consequent deft manipulating of inter-group rivalries, Corps officials on the scene played decisive roles in the preservation of domestic tranquility on many a far-flung world. At Fust, Ambassador Magnan forged to the van in the exercise of the technique . . .

Vol VII, reel 43. 487 A. E. (AD 2948)

ACROSS THE TABLE from Retief, Ambassador Magnan, rustling a stiff sheet of parchment, looked grave.

"This aide memoire," he said, "was just handed to me by the Cultural Attaché. It's the third on the subject this week. It refers to the matter of sponsorship of Youth groups."

"Some youths," Retief said. "Average age: seventy-five."

"The Fustians are a long-lived people," Magnan snapped. "These matters are relative. At seventy-five, a male Fustian is at a trying age."

"That's right; he'll try anything in the hope it will maim somebody."

"Precisely the problem," Magnan replied. "But the Youth Movement is the important news in today's political situation here on Fust, and sponsorship of Youth groups is a shrewd stroke on the part of the Terrestrial Embassy. At my suggestion, well nigh every member of the mission has leaped at the opportunity to score a few p— that is, to cement relations with this emergent power group: the leaders of the future. You, Retief, as Counselor, are the outstanding exception."

"I'm not convinced these hoodlums need my help in organizing their rumbles," Retief said. "Now, if you have a proposal for a pest control group—"

"To the Fustians, this is no jesting matter," Magnan cut in. "This group," he glanced at the paper, "known as the Sexual, Cultural and Athletic Recreational Society, or SCARS, for short, has been awaiting sponorship for a matter of weeks now."

"Meaning they want someone to buy them a clubhouse, uniforms, equipment, and anything else they need to plot against the peace in style," Retief said.

"If we don't act promptly, the Groaci embassy may well anticipate us. They're very active here."

"That's an idea," said Retief, "let 'em. After a while they'll be broke—instead of us."

"Nonsense. The group requires a sponsor. I can't actually order you to step forward. However . . ." Magnan let the sentence hang in the air. Retief raised one eyebrow.

"For a minute there," he said, "I thought you were going to make a positive statement."

Magnan leaned back, lacing his fingers over his stomach. "I don't think you'll find a diplomat of my experience doing anything so naive," he said.

"I like the adult Fustians," said Retief. "Too bad they have to lug half a ton of horn around on their backs. I wonder if surgery—"

"Great heavens, Retief," Magnan spluttered. "I'm amazed that even you would bring up a matter of such delicacy. A race's unfortunate physical characteristics are hardly a fit matter for Terrestrial curiosity."

"Well, I've only been here a month. But it's been my experience, Mr. Ambassador, that few people are above improving on nature; otherwise you, for example, would be tripping over your beard."

Magnan shuddered. "Please—never mention the idea to a Fustian."

Retief stood. "My own program for the day includes going over to the dockyards. There are some features of this new passenger liner the Fustians are putting together that I want to look into. With your permission, Mr. Ambassador. . . ?"

Magnan snorted. "Your preoccupation with the trivial disturbs me, Retief. More interest in substantive matters—such as working with youth groups—would create a far better impression."

"Before getting too involved with these groups, it might be a good idea to find out a little more about them," Retief said. "Who organizes them? There are three strong political parties here on Fust; what's the alignment of this SCARS organization?"

"You forget, these are merely teen-agers, so to speak," Magnan said. "Politics mean nothing to them . . . yet."

"Then there are the Groaci. Why their passionate interest in a two-horse world like Fust? Normally they're concerned with nothing but business; and what has Fust got that they could use?"

"You may rule out the commercial aspect in this instance," said Magnan. "Fust possesses a vigorous steel-age manufacturing economy. The Groaci are barely ahead of them."

"Barely," said Retief. "Just over the line into crude atomics . . . like fission bombs."

Magnan, shaking his head, turned back to his papers. "What market exists for such devices on a world at peace?" he said. "I suggest you address your attention to the less spectacular but more rewarding work of insinuating yourself into the social patterns of the local youth."

"I've considered the matter," Retief said, "and before I meet any of the local youth socially I want to get myself a good blackjack."

Retief left the sprawling bungalow-type building that housed the chancery of the Terrestrial Embassy, hailed one of the ponderous slow-moving Fustian flat-cars, and leaned back against the wooden guard rail as the heavy vehicle trundled through the city toward the looming gantries of the shipyards. It was a cool morning with a light breeze carrying the fish odor of Fustian dwellings across the broad cobbled avenue. A few mature Fustians lumbered heavily along in the shade of the low buildings, audibly wheezing under the burden of their immense carapaces. Among them, shell-less youths trotted briskly on scaly stub legs. The driver of the flat-car, a labor-caste Fustian with his guild colors emblazoned on his back, heaved at the tiller, swung the unwieldy conveyance through the shipyard gates, and creaked to a halt.

"Thus I come to the shipyard with frightful speed," he said in Fustian. "Well I know the way of the naked-backs, who move always in haste."

Retief, climbing down, handed him a coin. "You

should take up professional racing," he said. "Dare-devil."

Retief crossed the littered yard and tapped at the door of a rambling shed. Boards creaked inside, then the door swung back. A gnarled ancient with tarnished facial scales and a weathered carapace peered out at Retief.

"Long may you sleep," Retief said. "I'd like to take a look around, if you don't mind. I understand you're laying the bed-plate for your new liner today."

"May you dream of the deeps," the old fellow mumbled. He waved a stumpy arm toward a group of shell-less Fustians standing by a massive hoist. "The youths know more of bed-plates than do I, who but tend the place of papers."

"I know how you feel, old-timer," Retief said. "That sounds like the story of my life. Among your papers do you have a set of plans for the vessel? I understand it's to be a passenger liner."

The oldster nodded. He shuffled to a drawing file, rummaged, pulled out a sheaf of curled prints, and spread them on the table. Retief stood silently, running a finger over the uppermost drawing, tracing lines . . .

"What does the naked-back here?" a deep voice barked behind Retief. He turned. A heavy-faced Fustian youth, wrapped in a mantle, stood at the open door. Beady yellow eyes set among fine scales bored into Retief.

"I came to take a look at your new liner," said Retief.

"We need no prying foreigners here," the youth snapped. His eye fell on the drawings; he hissed in anger.

"Doddering hulk!" he snapped at the ancient, moving toward them. "May you toss in nightmares! Put aside the plans!"

"My mistake," Retief said. "I didn't know this was a secret project."

The youth hesitated. "It is not a secret," he muttered. "Why should it be a secret?"

"You tell me."

The youth worked his jaws and rocked his head from side to side in the Fustian gesture of uncertainty. "There is nothing to conceal," he said. "We merely construct a passenger liner."

"Then you don't mind if I look over the drawings," Retief said. "Who knows, maybe some day I'll want to reserve a suite for the trip out."

The youth turned and disappeared. Retief grinned at the oldster. "Went for his big brother, I guess," he said. "I have a feeling I won't get to study these in peace here. Mind if I copy them?"

"Willingly, light-footed one," said the old Fustian. "And mine is the shame for the discourtesy of youth."

Retief took out a tiny camera, flipped a copying lens in place, leafed through the drawings, clicking the shutter.

"A plague on these youths," said the oldster. "They grow more virulent day by day."

"Why don't you elders clamp down?"

"Agile are they and we are slow of foot. And this unrest is new; unknown in my youth was such insolence."

"The police—"

"Bah," the ancient rumbled. "None have we worthy of the name, nor have we needed them before now."

"What's behind it?"

"They have found leaders. The spiv, Slock, is one. And I fear they plot mischief." He pointed to the window. "They come, and a soft-one with them."

Retief, pocketing the camera, glanced out the window. A pale-featured Groacian with an ornately decorated crest stood with the youths, who eyed the hut, then started toward it.

"That's the military attaché of the Groaci Embassy," Retief said. "I wonder what he and the boys are cooking up together?"

"Naught that augurs well for the dignity of Fust," the oldster rumbled. "Flee, agile one, while I engage their attentions."

"I was just leaving," Retief said. "Which way out?"

"The rear door," the Fustian gestured with a stubby member. "Rest well, stranger on these shores," he said, moving to the entrance.

"Same to you, pop," said Retief. "And thanks."

He eased through the narrow back entrance, waited until voices were raised at the front of the shed, then strolled off toward the gate.

It was an hour along in the second dark of the third cycle when Retief left the Embassy technical library and crossed the corridor to his office. He flipped on a light and found a note tucked under a paperweight:

"Retief: I shall expect your attendance at the IAS dinner at first dark of the fourth cycle. There will be a brief but, I hope, impressive sponsorship ceremony for the SCARS group, with full press coverage, arrangements

*for which I have managed to complete in
spite of your intransigence."*

Retief snorted and glanced at his watch: less
than three hours. Just time to creep home by
flat-car, dress in ceremonial uniform, and creep
back.

Outside he flagged a lumbering bus, stationed
himself in a corner of it, and watched the yellow
sun, Beta, rise above the low skyline. The nearby
sea was at high tide now, under the pull of the
major sun and the three moons, and the stiff breeze
carried a mist of salt spray. Retief turned up his
collar against the dampness. In half an hour he
would be perspiring under the vertical rays of a
first-noon sun, but the thought failed to keep the
chill off.

Two youths clambered up on the moving platform and walked purposefully toward Retief. He
moved off the rail, watching them, his weight
balanced.

"That's close enough, kids," he said. "Plenty of
room on this scow; no need to crowd up."

"There are certain films," the lead Fustian muttered. His voice was unusually deep for a Youth.
He was wrapped in a heavy cloak and moved
awkwardly. His adolescence was nearly at an end,
Retief guessed.

"I told you once," Retief said. "Don't crowd
me."

The two stepped close, their slit mouths snapping in anger. Retief put out a foot, hooked it
behind the scaly leg of the over-age juvenile, and
threw his weight against the cloaked chest. The
clumsy Fustian tottered, then fell heavily. Retief
was past him and off the flat-car before the other

youth had completed his vain lunge toward the spot Retief had occupied. The Terrestrial waved cheerfully at the pair, hopped aboard another vehicle, and watched his would-be assailants lumber down off their car and move heavily off, their tiny heads twisted to follow his retreating figure.

So they wanted the film? Retief reflected, thumbing a cigar alight. They were a little late. He had already filed it in the Embassy vault, after running a copy for the reference files. And a comparison of the drawings with those of the obsolete Mark XXXV battle cruiser used two hundred years earlier by the Concordiat Naval Arm showed them to be almost identical—gun emplacements and all. And the term obsolete was a relative one. A ship which had been outmoded in the armories of the Galactic Powers could still be king of the walk in the Eastern Arm.

But how had these two known of the film? There had been no one present but himself and the old-timer—and Retief was willing to bet the elderly Fustian hadn't told them anything.

At least not willingly . . .

Retief frowned, dropped the cigar over the side, waited until the flat-car negotiated a mud-wallow, then swung down and headed for the shipyard.

The door, hinges torn loose, had been propped loosely back in position. Retief looked around at the battered interior of the shed. The old fellow had put up a struggle.

There were deep drag-marks in the dust behind the building. Retief followed them across the yard. They disappeared under the steel door of a warehouse.

Retief glanced around. Now, at the mid-hour of the fourth cycle, the workmen were heaped along the edge of the refreshment pond, deep in their siesta. Taking a multi-bladed tool from his pocket, Retief tried various fittings in the lock; it snicked open and he eased the door aside far enough to enter.

Heaped bales loomed before him. Snapping on the tiny lamp in the handle of the combination tool, Retief looked over the pile. One stack seemed out of alignment—and the dust had been scraped from the floor before it. He pocketed the light, climbed up on the bales, and looked over into a ring of bundles. The aged Fustian lay inside the ring, a heavy sack tied over his head. Retief dropped down beside him, sawed at the tough twine, and pulled the sack free.

"It's me, old fellow," he said, "the nosy stranger. Sorry I got you into this."

The oldster threshed his gnarled legs, rocked slightly, then fell back. "A curse on the cradle that rocked their infant slumbers," he rumbled. "But place me back on my feet and I hunt down the youth Slock though he flee to the bottom-most muck of the Sea of Torments."

"How am I going to get you out of here? Maybe I'd better get some help."

"Nay. The perfidious youths abound here," said the old Fustian. "It would be your life."

"I doubt if they'd go that far."

"Would they not?" The Fustian stretched his neck. "Cast your light here. But for the toughness of my hide . . ."

Retief put the beam of the light on the leathery neck. A great smear of thick purplish blood welled

from a ragged cut. The oldster chuckled: a sound
like a seal coughing.

"Traitor they called me. For long they sawed at
me—in vain. Then they trussed me and dumped
me here. They think to return with weapons to
complete the task."

"Weapons? I thought it was illegal—"

"Their evil genius, the Soft One," the Fustian
said, "he would provide fuel to the Fire-Devil."

"The Groaci again," Retief said. "I wonder what
their angle is."

"And I must confess: I told them of you, ere I
knew their full intentions. Much can I tell you of
their doings. But first, I pray: the block and tackle."

Retief found the hoist where the Fustian directed him, maneuvered it into position, hooked
onto the edge of the carapace, and hauled away.
The immense Fustian rose slowly, teetered . . .
then flopped on his chest. Slowly he got to his
feet.

"My name is Whonk, fleet one," he said. "My
cows are yours."

"Thanks. I'm Retief. I'd like to meet the girls
some time. But right now, let's get out of here."

Whonk leaned his bulk against the ponderous
stacks of baled kelp, bull-dozing them aside. "Slow
am I to anger," he said, "but implacable in my
wrath. Slock, beware . . ."

"Hold it," said Retief suddenly. He sniffed.
"What's that odor?" He flashed the light around,
playing it over a dry stain on the floor. He knelt
and sniffed at the spot.

"What kind of cargo was stacked here, Whonk?
And where is it now?"

Whonk considered. "There were drums," he

said. "Four of them, quite small, painted an evil green—the property of the Soft Ones, the Groaci. They lay here a day and a night. At full dark of the first period they came with stevedores and loaded them aboard the barge *Moss Rock*."

"The VIP boat. Who's scheduled to use it?"

"I know not. But what matters this? Let us discuss cargo movements after I have settled a score with certain youths."

"We'd better follow this up first, Whonk. There's only one substance I know of that's transported in drums and smells like that blot on the floor. That's titanite: the hottest explosive this side of a uranium pile."

Beta was setting as Retief, with Whonk puffing at his heels, came up to the sentry box beside the gangway leading to the plush interior of the Official Barge *Moss Rock*.

"A sign of the times," Whonk said, glancing inside the empty shelter. "A guard should stand here, but I see him not. Doubtless he crept away to sleep."

"Let's go aboard, and take a look around."

They entered the ship. Soft lights glowed in utter silence. A rough box stood on the floor, rollers and pry-bars beside it—a discordant note in the muted luxury of the setting. Whonk rummaged through its contents.

"Curious," he said. "What means this?" He held up a stained Fustian cloak of orange and green, a metal bracelet, and a stack of papers.

"Orange and green," Retief muttered. "Whose colors are those?"

"I know not. . . ." Whonk glanced at the armband. "But this is lettered." He passed the metal band to Retief.

"SCARS," Retief read. He looked at Whonk. "It seems to me I've heard the name before," he murmured. "Let's get back to the Embassy—fast."

Back on the ramp Retief heard a sound . . . and turned in time to duck the charge of a hulking Fustian youth who thundered past him, and fetched up against the broad chest of Whonk, who locked him in a warm embrace.

"Nice catch, Whonk. Where'd he sneak out of?"

"The lout hid there by the storage bin," Whonk rumbled. The captive youth thumped his fists and toes futilely against the oldster's carapace.

"Hang on to him," Retief said. "He looks like the biting kind."

"No fear. Clumsy I am, yet I am not without strength."

"Ask him where the titanite is tucked away."

"Speak, witless grub," Whonk growled, "lest I tweak you in two."

The youth gurgled.

"Better let up before you make a mess of him," Retief said.

Whonk lifted the youth clear of the floor, then flung him down with a thump that made the ground quiver. The younger Fustian glared up at the elder, his mouth snapping.

"This one was among those who trussed me and hid me away for the killing," said Whonk. "In his repentance he will tell all to his elder."

"He's the same one that tried to strike up an acquaintance with me on the bus," Retief said. "He gets around."

The youth, scrambling to his hands and knees,

scuttled for freedom. Retief planted a foot on the dragging cloak; it ripped free. He stared at the bare back of the Fustian.

"By the Great Egg!" Whonk exclaimed, tripping the captive as he tried to rise. "This is no youth! His carapace has been taken from him."

Retief looked at the scarred back. "I thought he looked a little old. But I thought—"

"This is not possible," Whonk said wonderingly. "The great nerve trunks are deeply involved; not even the cleverest surgeon could excise the carapace and leave the patient living."

"It looks like somebody did the trick. But let's take this boy with us and get out of here. His folks may come home."

"Too late," said Whonk. Retief turned. Three youths came from behind the sheds.

"Well," Retief said. "It looks like the SCARS are out in force tonight. Where's your pal?" he said to the advancing trio, "the sticky little bird with the eye-stalks? Back at his Embassy, leaving you suckers holding the bag, I'll bet."

"Shelter behind me, Retief," said Whonk.

"Go get 'em, old-timer," Retief stooped and picked up one of the pry-bars. "I'll jump around and distract them."

Whonk let out a whistling roar and charged for the immature Fustians. They fanned out . . . one tripped, sprawling on his face. Retief, whirling the metal bar that he had thrust between the Fustian's legs, slammed it against the skull of another, who shook his head, then turned on Retief . . . and bounced off the steel hull of the *Moss Rock* as Whonk took him in full charge.

Retief used the bar on another head; his third

blow laid the Fustian on the pavement, oozing purple. The other two club members departed hastily, dented but still mobile.

Retief leaned on his club, breathing hard. "Tough heads these kids have got. I'm tempted to chase those two lads down, but I've got another errand to run. I don't know who the Groaci intended to blast, but I have a suspicion somebody of importance was scheduled for a boatride in the next few hours, and three drums of titanite is enough to vaporize this tub and everyone aboard her."

"The plot is foiled," said Whonk. "But what reason did they have?"

"The Groaci are behind it. I have an idea the SCARS didn't know about this gambit."

"Which of these is the leader?" asked Whonk. He prodded a fallen youth. "Arise, dreaming one."

"Never mind him, Whonk. We'll tie these two up and leave them here. I know where to find the boss."

A stolid-looking crowd filled the low-ceilinged banquet hall. Retief scanned the tables for the pale blobs of Terrestrial faces, dwarfed by the giant armored bodies of the Fustians. Across the room Magnan fluttered a hand. Retief headed toward him. A low-pitched vibration filled the air, the rumble of sub-sonic Fustian music.

Retief slid into his place beside Magnan. "Sorry to be late, Mr. Ambassador."

"I'm honored that you chose to appear at all," Magnan said coldly. He turned back to the Fustian on his left.

"Ah, yes, Mr. Minister," he said. "Charming, most charming. So joyous."

The Fustian looked at him, beady-eyed. "It is the Lament of Hatching," he said, "our National Dirge."

"Oh," said Magnan, "how interesting. Such a pleasing balance of instruments."

"It is a droon solo," said the Fustian, eyeing the Terrestrial Ambassador suspiciously.

"Why don't you just admit you can't hear it," Retief whispered loudly. "And if I may interrupt a moment—"

Magnan cleared his throat. "Now that our Mr. Retief has arrived, perhaps we could rush right along to the sponsorship ceremonies . . ."

"This group," said Retief, leaning across Magnan to speak to the Fustian, "the SCARS . . . how much do you know about them, Mr. Minister?"

"Nothing at all," the huge Fustian elder rumbled. "For my taste, all youths should be kept penned with the livestock until they grow a carapace to tame their irresponsibility."

"We mustn't lose sight of the importance of channeling youthful energies," said Magnan.

"Labor gangs," said the minister. "In my youth we were indentured to the dredge-masters. I myself drew a muck-sledge."

"But in these modern times," put in Retief, "surely it's incumbent on us to make happy these golden hours."

The minister snorted. "Last week I had a golden hour: they set upon me and pelted me with over-ripe dung-fruit."

"But this was merely a manifestation of normal youthful frustrations," cried Magnan. "Their essential tenderness—"

"You'd not find a tender spot on that lout yonder," the minister said, pointing with a fork at a newly arrived youth, "if you drilled boreholes and blasted."

"Why, that's our guest of honor," said Magnan, "a fine young fellow. Slop I believe his name is—"

"Slock," said Retief. "Nine feet of armor-plated orneriness. And—"

Magnan rose, tapping on his glass. The Fustians winced at the, to them, supersonic vibrations, and looked at each other muttering. Magnan tapped louder. The minister drew in his head, his eyes closed. Some of the Fustians rose and tottered for the doors; the noise level rose. Magnan redoubled his efforts. The glass broke with a clatter, and green wine gushed on the tablecloth.

"What in the name of the Great Egg," the minister muttered. He blinked, breathing deeply.

"Oh, forgive me," Magnan blurted, dabbing at the wine.

"Too bad the glass gave out," Retief said. "In another minute you'd have cleared the hall—and then maybe I could have gotten a word in. You see, Mr. Minister," he said, turning to the Fustian, "there is a matter you should know about. . . ."

"Your attention, please," Magnan said, rising. "I see that our fine young guest of honor has arrived, and I hope that the remainder of his committee will be along in a moment. It is my pleasure to announce that our Mr. Retief has had the good fortune to win out in the keen bidding for the pleasure of sponsoring this lovely group, and—"

Retief tugged at Magnan's sleeve. "Don't introduce me yet," he said. "I want to appear suddenly— more dramatic, you know."

"Well," Magnan murmured, glancing down at

Retief, "I'm gratified to see you entering into the spirit of the event at last." He turned his attention back to the assembled guests. "If our honored guest will join me on the rostrum . . ." he said. "The gentlemen of the press may want to catch a few shots of the presentation."

Magnan moved from his place, made his way forward, stepped up on the low platform at the center of the wide room, took his place beside the robed Fustian youth, and beamed at the cameras.

"How gratifying it is to take this opportunity to express once more the great pleasure we have in sponsoring SCARS," Magnan said, talking slowly for the benefit of the scribbling reporters. "We'd like to think that in our modest way we're to be a part of all that the SCARS achieve during the years ahead. . . ."

Magnan paused as a huge Fustian elder heaved his bulk up the two low steps to the rostrum and approached the guest of honor. He watched as the newcomer paused behind Slock, who was busy returning the stares of the spectators and did not notice the new arrival.

Retief pushed through the crowd and stepped up to face the Fustian youth. Slock stared at him, drawing back.

"You know me, Slock," Retief said loudly. "An old fellow named Whonk told you about me, just before you tried to saw off his head, remember? It was when I came out to take a look at that battle cruiser you're building."

With a bellow Slock reached for Retief—and choked off in mid-cry as Whonk pinioned him from behind, lifting the youth clear of the floor.

"Glad you reporters happened along," Retief

said to the gaping newsmen. "Slock here had a deal with a sharp operator from the Groaci Embassy. The Groaci were to supply the necessary hardware and Slock, as foreman at the shipyards, was to see that everything was properly installed. The next step, I assume, would have been a local take-over, followed by a little interplanetary war on Flamenco or one of the other nearby worlds . . . for which the Groaci would be glad to supply plenty of ammo."

Magnan found his tongue. "Are you mad, Retief?" he screeched. "This group was vouched for by the Ministry of Youth."

"That Ministry's overdue for a purge," Retief said. He turned back to Slock. "I wonder if you were in on the little diversion that was planned for today. When the *Moss Rock* blew, a variety of clues were to be planted where they'd be easy to find . . . with SCARS written all over them. The Groaci would thus have neatly laid the whole affair squarely at the door of the Terrestrial Embassy . . . whose sponsorship of the SCARS had received plenty of publicity."

"The *Moss Rock?*" Magnan said. "But that was— Retief! This is idiotic. The SCARS themselves were scheduled to go on a cruise tomorrow."

Slock roared suddenly, twisting violently. Whonk teetered, his grip loosened . . . and Slock pulled free and was off the platform, butting his way through the milling oldsters on the dining room floor. Magnan watched, openmouthed.

"The Groaci were playing a double game, as usual," Retief said. "They intended to dispose of these lads after they got things under way."

"Well, don't stand there," Magnan yelped. "Do

something! If Slop is the ringleader of a delin-
quent gang—" He moved to give chase himself.

Retief grabbed his arm. "Don't jump down
there," he called above the babble of talk. "You'd
have as much chance of getting through there as a
jack rabbit through a threshing contest. Where's a
phone?"

Ten minutes later the crowd had thinned slightly.
"We can get through now," Whonk called. "This
way." He lowered himself to the floor and bulled
through to the exit. Flash bulbs popped. Retief
and Magnan followed in Whonk's wake.

In the lounge Retief grabbed the phone, waited
for the operator, and gave a code letter. No reply.
He tried another.

"No good," he said after a full minute had passed.
He slammed the phone back in its niche. "Let's
grab a cab."

In the street the blue sun, Alpha, peered like an
arc light under a low cloud layer. Flat shadows lay
across the mud of the avenue. The three mounted
a passing flat-car. Whonk squatted, resting the
weight of his immense shell on the heavy plank
flooring.

"Would that I, too, could lose this burden, as
has the false youth we bludgeoned aboard the
Moss Rock," he sighed. "Soon will I be forced into
retirement; and a mere keeper of a place of papers
such as I will rate no more than a slab on the
public strand, with once-daily feedings. Even for a
man of high position retirement is no pleasure. A
slab in the Park of Monuments is little better. A
dismal outlook for one's next thousand years."

"You two continue on to the police station,"

Retief said. "I want to play a hunch. But don't take too long. I may be painfully right."

"What—?" Magnan started.

"As you wish, Retief," Whonk said.

The flat-car trundled past the gate to the ship-yard and Retief jumped down and headed at a run for the VIP boat. The guard post still stood vacant. The two youths whom he and Whonk had left trussed were gone.

"That's the trouble with a peaceful world," Retief muttered. "No police protection." Stepping down from the lighted entry, he took up a position behind the sentry box. Alpha rose higher, shedding a glaring white light without heat. Retief shivered.

There was a sound in the near entrance, like two elephants colliding. Retief looked toward the gate. His giant acquaintance, Whonk, had reappeared and was grappling with a hardly less massive opponent. A small figure became visible in the melee, scuttled for the gate, was headed off by the battling titans, turned and made for the opposite side of the shipyard. Retief waited, jumped out and gathered in the fleeing Groacian.

"Well, Yith," he said, "how's tricks. . . ? you should pardon the expression."

"Release me, Retief!" the pale-featured creature lisped, his throat bladder pulsating in agitation. "The behemoths vie for the privilege of dismembering me."

"I know how they feel. I'll see what I can do . . . for a price."

"I appeal to you," Yith whispered hoarsely, "as a fellow diplomat, a fellow alien, a fellow soft-back."

"Why don't you appeal to Slock, as fellow conspirator?" Retief said. "Now keep quiet . . . and you may get out of this alive."

The heavier of the two struggling Fustians threw the other to the ground. The smaller Fustian lay on its back, helpless.

"That's Whonk, still on his feet," Retief said. "I wonder who he's caught—and why."

Whonk came toward the *Moss Rock* dragging the supine Fustian. Retief thrust Yith down well out of sight behind the sentry box. "Better sit tight, Yith. Don't try to sneak off; I can outrun you. Stay here and I'll see what I can do." Stepping out, he hailed Whonk.

Puffing like a steam engine, Whonk pulled up before him. "Hail, Retief!" he panted. "You followed a hunch; I did the same. I saw something strange in this one when we passed him on the avenue. I watched, followed him here. Look! It is Slock, strapped into a dead carapace! Now many things become clear."

Retief whistled. "So the youths aren't all as young as they look. Somebody's been holding out on the rest of you Fustians."

"The soft one," Whonk said. "You laid him by the heels, Retief. I saw. Produce him now."

"Hold on a minute, Whonk. It won't do you any good to—"

Whonk winked broadly. "I must take my revenge!" he roared. "I shall test the texture of the Soft One! His pulped remains will be scoured up by the ramp-washers and mailed home in bottles."

Retief whirled at a sound, caught up with the scuttling Yith fifty feet away, and hauled him back to Whonk.

"It's up to you, Whonk," he said. "I know how important ceremonial revenge is to you Fustians."

"Mercy!" Yith hissed, his eye-stalks whipping in distress. "I claim diplomatic immunity."

"No diplomat am I," Whonk rumbled. "Let me see; suppose I start with one of those obscenely active eyes." He reached . . .

"I have an idea," Retief said brightly. "Do you suppose—just this once—you could forego the ceremonial revenge if Yith promised to arrange for a Groacian Surgical Mission to de-carapace you elders?"

"But," Whonk protested, "those eyes; what a pleasure to pluck them, one by one—"

"Yes," Yith hissed, "I swear it; our most expert surgeons . . . platoons of them, with the finest of equipment."

"I have dreamed of how it would be to sit on this one, to feel him squash beneath my bulk. . . ."

"Light as a whistle feather shall you dance," Yith whispered. "Shell-less shall you spring in the joy of renewed youth. . . ."

"Maybe just one eye," Whonk said. "That would leave him four. . . ."

"Be a sport," said Retief.

"Well."

"It's a deal then," Retief said. "Yith, on your word as a diplomat, an alien, and a soft-back, you'll set up the mission. Groaci surgical skill is an export that will net you more than armaments. It will be a whistle feather in your cap—if you bring it off. And in return, Whonk won't sit on you. In addition, I won't prefer charges against you of interference in the internal affairs of a free world."

Behind Whonk there was a movement. Slock,

wriggling free of the borrowed carapace, struggled to his feet . . . in time for Whonk to seize him, lift him high, and head for the entry to the *Moss Rock*.

"Hey," Retief called. "Where are you going?"

"I would not deny this one his reward," Whonk called. "He hoped to cruise in luxury; so be it."

"Hold on," Retief said. "That tub is loaded with titanite!"

"Stand not in my way, Retief. For this one in truth owes me a vengeance."

Retief watched as the immense Fustian bore his giant burden up the ramp and disappeared within the ship.

"I guess Whonk means business," he said to Yith, who hung in his grasp, all five eyes goggling. "And he's a little too big for me to stop, once he sets his mind on something. But maybe he's just throwing a scare into him."

Whonk reappeared, alone, and climbed down.

"What did you do with him?" Retief said.

"We had best withdraw," Whonk said. "The killing radius of the drive is fifty yards."

"You mean—"

"The controls are set for Groac. Long may he sleep."

"It was quite a bang," Retief said, "but I guess you saw it too."

"No, confound it," Magnan said. "When I remonstrated with Hulk, or Whelk—"

"Whonk."

"—the ruffian thrust me into an alley, bound in my own cloak. I'll most certainly mention the indignity in a note to the Minister." He jotted on a pad.

"How about the surgical mission?"

"A most generous offer," Magnan said. "Frankly, I was astonished. I think perhaps we've judged the Groaci too harshly."

"I hear the Ministry of Youth has had a rough morning of it," Retief said. "And a lot of rumors are flying to the effect that Youth Groups are on the way out."

Magnan cleared his throat and shuffled papers. "I—ah—have explained to the press that last night's ahh . . ."

"Fiasco."

"—affair was necessary in order to place the culprits in an untenable position. Of course, as to the destruction of the VIP vessel and the presumed death of the fellow, Slop—"

"The Fustians understand," Retief said. "Whonk wasn't kidding about ceremonial vengeance. Yith was lucky: he hadn't actually drawn blood. Then no amount of dickering would have saved him."

"The Groaci have been guilty of gross misuse of diplomatic privilege," Magnan said. "I think that a note—or perhaps an *aide memoire:* less formal. . . ."

"The *Moss Rock* was bound for Groac," Retief said. "She was already in her transit orbit when she blew. The major fragments should arrive on schedule in a month or so. It should provide quite a meteorite display. I think that should be all the aid the Groaci's *memoires* will need to keep their tentacles off Fust."

"But diplomatic usage—"

"Then, too, the less that's put in writing, the less they can blame you for, if anything goes wrong."

"There's that, of course," Magnan said, his lips pursed. "Now you're thinking constructively, Retief. We may make a diplomat of you yet." He smiled expansively.

"Maybe. But I refuse to let it depress me." Retief stood up. "I'm taking a few weeks off . . . if you have no objections, Mr. Ambassador. My pal Whonk wants to show me an island down south where the fishing is good."

"But there are some extremely important matters coming up," Magnan said. "We're planning to sponsor Senior Citizen Groups."

"Count me out. Groups give me an itch."

"Why, what an astonishing remark, Retief. After all, we diplomats are ourselves a group."

"Uh, huh," Retief said. "That's what I mean."

Magnan sat quietly, his mouth open, and watched as Retief stepped into the hall and closed the door gently behind him.

Policy

. . . No jackstraws to be swayed by superficial appearances, dedicated career field personnel of the Corps unflaggingly administered the enlightened concepts evolved at Corps HQ by high-level deep-think teams toiling unceasingly in underground caverns to weld the spirit of Inter-Being amity. Never has the efficacy of close cultural rapport, coupled with Mission teamwork, been better displayed than in the loyal performance of Administrative Assistant Yolanda Meuhl, Acting Consul at GROAC, in maintaining the Corps posture laid down by her predecessor, Consul Whaffle . . .

Vol VII, reel 98. 488 A. E. (AD 2949)

"THE CONSUL for the Terrestrial States," Retief said, "presents his compliments, et cetera, to the Ministry of Culture of the Groacian Autonomy, and, with reference to the Ministry's invitation to attend a recital of interpretive grimacing, has the honor to express regret that he will be unable—"

"You can't turn down this invitation," Administrative Assistant Meuhl said flatly. "I'll make that 'accepts with pleasure'."

Retief exhaled a plume of cigar smoke.

"Miss Meuhl," he said, "in the past couple of weeks I've sat through six light concerts, four attempts at chamber music, and God knows how many assorted folk-art festivals. I've been tied up every off-duty hour since I got here."

"You can't offend the Groaci," Miss Meuhl said sharply. "Consul Whaffle would never have—"

"Whaffle left here three months ago," Retief said, "leaving me in charge."

"Well," Miss Meuhl said, snapping off the

112

dictyper. "I'm sure I don't know what excuse I can give the Minister."

"Never mind the excuses. Just tell him I won't be there." He stood up.

"Are you leaving the office?" Miss Meuhl adjusted her glasses. "I have some important letters here for your signature."

"I don't recall dictating any letters today, Miss Meuhl," Retief said, pulling on a light cape.

"I wrote them for you. They're just as Consul Whaffle would have wanted them."

"Did you write all Whaffle's letters for him, Miss Meuhl?"

"Consul Whaffle was an extremely busy man," Miss Muehl said stiffly. "He had complete confidence in me."

"Since I'm cutting out the culture from now on, I won't be so busy."

"Well! May I ask where you'll be if something comes up?"

"I'm going over to the Foreign Office Archives."

Miss Meuhl blinked behind thick lenses. "Whatever for?"

Retief looked at her thoughtfully. "You've been here on Groac for four years, Miss Meuhl. What was behind the coup d'etat that put the present government in power?"

"I'm sure I haven't pried into—"

"What about that Terrestrial cruiser, the one that disappeared out this way about ten years back?"

"Mr. Retief, those are just the sort of questions we avoid with the Groaci. I certainly hope you're not thinking of openly intruding—"

"Why?"

"The Groaci are a very sensitive race. They

don't welcome outworlders raking up things. They've been gracious enough to let us live down the fact that Terrestrials subjected them to deep humiliation on one occasion."

"You mean when we came looking for the cruiser?"

"I, for one, am ashamed of the high-handed tactics that were employed, grilling these innocent people as though they were criminals. We try never to reopen that wound, Mr. Retief."

"They never found the cruiser, did they?"

"Certainly not on Groac."

Retief nodded. "Thanks, Miss Meuhl," he said. "I'll be back before you close the office." Miss Meuhl's thin face was set in lines of grim disapproval as he closed the door.

Peering through the small grilled window, the pale-featured Groacian vibrated his throat-bladder in a distressed bleat.

"Not to enter the Archives," he said in his faint voice. "The denial of permission. The deep regret of the Archivist."

"The importance of my task here," Retief said, enunciating the glottal language with difficulty. "My interest in local history."

"The impossibility of access to outworlders. To depart quietly."

"The necessity that I enter."

"The specific instructions of the Archivist." The Groacian's voice rose to a whisper. "To insist no longer. To give up this idea!"

"Okay, skinny, I know when I'm licked," Retief said in Terran. "To keep your nose clean."

Outside, Retief stood for a moment looking across at the deeply carved windowless stucco facades

lining the street, then started off in the direction
of the Terrestrial Consulate General. The few
Groacians on the street eyed him furtively, and
veered to avoid him as he passed. Flimsy high-
wheeled ground cars puffed silently along the re-
silient pavement. The air was clean and cool. At
the office Miss Meuhl would be waiting with another list of complaints. Retief studied the carving
over the open doorways along the street. An elaborate one picked out in pinkish paint seemed to
indicate the Groacian equivalent of a bar. Retief
went in.

A Groacian bartender dispensing clay pots of al-
coholic drink from the bar-pit at the center of the
room looked at Retief, then froze in mid-motion, a
metal tube poised over a waiting pot.

"A cooling drink," Retief said in Groacian, squat-
ting down at the edge of the pit. "To sample a true
Groacian beverage."

"Not to enjoy my poor offerings," the Groacian
mumbled. "A pain in the digestive sacs. To express regret."

"Not to worry," Retief replied. "To pour it out
and let me decide whether I like it."

"To be grappled in by peace-keepers for poison-
ing of . . . foreigners." The barkeep looked around
for support, but found none. The Groaci customers, eyes elsewhere, were drifting out.

"To get the lead out," Retief said, placing a
thick gold-piece in the dish provided. "To shake a
tentacle."

"To procure a cage," a thin voice called from the
sidelines. "To display the freak."

Retief turned. A tall Groacian vibrated his mandibles in a gesture of contempt. From his bluish

throat coloration it was apparent the creature was drunk.

"To choke in your upper sac," the bartender hissed, extending his eyes toward the drunk. "To keep silent, litter-mate of drones."

"To swallow your own poison, dispenser of vileness," the drunk whispered. "To find a proper cage for this zoo-piece." He waved toward Retief. "To show this one in the streets, like all freaks."

"Seen a lot of freaks like me, have you?" Retief asked interestedly.

"To speak intelligibly, malodorous outworlder," the drunk said. The barkeep whispered something and two customers came up to the drunk, took his arms, and helped him to the door.

"To get a cage," the drunk shrilled. "To keep the animals in their place . . ."

"I've changed my mind," Retief said to the bartender. "To be grateful as hell, but to have to hurry off now." He followed the drunk out the door. The other Groaci, releasing the heckler, hurried back inside. Retief looked at the weaving creature.

"To begone, freak," the Groacian whispered.

"To be pals," Retief said. "To be kind to dumb animals."

"To have you hauled away to a stockyard, ill-odored foreign livestock."

"Not to be angry, fragrant native," Retief said. "To permit me to chum with you."

"To flee before I take a cane to you!"

"To have a drink together."

"Not to endure such insolence." The Groacian advanced toward Retief. Retief backed away.

"To hold hands," he said. "To be buddies—"

The Groacian reached for him, but missed. A passer-by stepped around him, head down, and scuttled away. Retief, backing into the opening to a narrow cross-way, offered further verbal familiarities to the drunken local, who followed, furious. Retief stepped around him, seized his collar and yanked. The Groacian fell on his back. Retief stood over him. The downed native half rose; Retief put a foot against his chest and pushed.

"Not to be going anywhere for a few minutes," he said. "To stay right here and have a nice long talk."

"There you are!" Miss Meuhl said, eyeing Retief over her lenses. "There are two gentlemen waiting to see you. Groacian gentlemen."

"Government men, I imagine. Word travels fast." Retief pulled off his cape. "This saves me the trouble of paying another call at the Foreign Ministry."

"What have you been doing? They seem very upset, I don't mind telling you."

"I'm sure you don't. Come along—and bring an official recorder."

Two Groaci, wearing heavy-shields and elaborate crest ornaments, indicative of rank, rose as Retief entered the room. Neither offered a courteous snap of the mandibles, Retief noted; they were mad, all right.

"I am Fith, of the Terrestrial Desk, Ministry of Foreign Affairs," the taller Groacian said, in lisping Terran. "May I present Shluh, of the Internal Police."

"Sit down, gentlemen," Retief said. They resumed their seats. Miss Meuhl hovered nervously, then sat down on the edge of a chair.

"Oh, it's such a pleasure—" she began.

"Never mind that," Retief said. "These gentlemen didn't come here to sip tea today."

"True," Fith rasped. "Frankly, I have had a most disturbing report, Mr. Consul. I shall ask Shluh to recount it." He nodded to the police chief.

"One hour ago," Shluh said, "a Groacian national was brought to hospital suffering from serious contusions. Questioning of this individual revealed that he had been set upon and beaten by a foreigner; a Terrestrial, to be precise. Investigation by my Department indicates that the description of the culprit closely matches that of the Terrestrial Consul. . . ."

Miss Meuhl gasped audibly.

"Have you ever heard," Retief said, looking steadily at Fith, "of a Terrestrial cruiser, the *ISV Terrific*, which dropped from sight in this sector nine years ago?"

"Really!" Miss Meuhl exclaimed, rising. "I wash my hands—"

"Just keep that recorder going," Retief snapped.

"I'll not be a party—"

"You'll do as you're told, Miss Meuhl," Retief said quietly. "I'm telling you to make an official sealed record of this conversation."

Miss Meuhl sat down.

Fith puffed out his throat indignantly. "You reopen an old wound, Mr. Consul. It reminds us of certain illegal treatment at Terrestrial hands."

"Hogwash," Retief said. "That tune went over

with my predecessors, but it hits a sour note with me."

"All our efforts," Miss Meuhl said, "to live down that terrible episode; and you—"

"Terrible? I understand that a Terrestrial Peace Enforcer stood off Groac and sent a delegation down to ask questions. They got some funny answers and stayed on to dig around a little. After a week, they left. Somewhat annoying to you Groaci, if you were innocent—"

"*If!*" Miss Meuhl burst out.

"If, indeed," Fith said, his weak voice trembling. "I must protest your—"

"Save your protests, Fith. You have some explaining to do, and I don't think your story will be good enough."

"It is for you to explain; this person who was beaten—"

"Not beaten; just rapped a few times to loosen his memory."

"Then you admit—"

"It worked, too. He remembered lots of things, once he put his mind to it."

Fith rose; Shluh followed suit.

"I shall ask for your immediate recall, Mr. Consul. Were it not for your diplomatic immunity, I should—"

"Why did the Government fall, Fith, just after the Task Force paid its visit, and before the arrival of the first Terrestrial diplomatic mission?"

"This is an internal matter," Fith cried, in his faint Groacian voice. "The new regime has shown itself most amiable to you Terrestrials; it has outdone itself—"

"—to keep the Terrestrial Consul and his staff in

the dark," Retief said, "and the same goes for the few Terrestrial businessmen you've given visas. This continual round of culture; no social contacts outside the diplomatic circle; no travel permits to visit outlying districts or your satellite—"

"Enough!" Fith's mandibles quivered in distress. "I can talk no more of this matter."

"You'll talk to me, or there's be a squadron of Peace Enforcers here in five days to do the talking," Retief said.

"You can't—" Miss Meuhl gasped.

Retief turned a steady look on Miss Meuhl. She closed her mouth. The Groaci sat down.

"Answer me this one," Retief said, looking at Shluh. "A few years back—nine, to be exact—there was a little parade held here. Some curious-looking creatures were captured, and after being securely caged, were exhibited to the gentle Groacian public. Hauled through the streets. Very educational, no doubt. A highly cultural show.

"Funny thing about these animals: they wore clothes, seemed to communicate with each other. Altogether a very amusing exhibit.

"Tell me, Shluh, what happened to those six Terrestrials after the parade was over?"

Fith made a choked noise, then spoke rapidly to Shluh in Groacian. Shluh, retracting his eyes, shrank down in his chair. Miss Meuhl opened her mouth, then closed it.

"How did they die?" Retief snapped. "Did you cut their throats, shoot them, bury them alive? What amusing end did you figure out for them? Research, maybe. Cut them open to see what made them yell. . . ."

"No," Fith gasped. "I must correct this terrible false impression at once."

"False impression, hell," Relief said. "They were Terrans; a simple narco-interrogation would get that out of any Groacian who saw the parade."

"Yes," Fith said weakly. "It is true, they were Terrestrials. But there was no killing—"

"They're alive?"

"Alas, no. They . . . died."

"I see," Retief said. "They died."

"We tried to keep them alive, of course; but we did not know what foods—"

"Didn't take the trouble to find out."

"They fell ill," Fith said. "One by one . . ."

"We'll deal with that question later," Retief said. "Right now, I want more information. Where did you get them? Where did you hide the ship? What happened to the rest of the crew? Did they 'fall ill' before the big parade?"

"There were no more! Absolutely, I assure you!"

"Killed in the crash landing?"

"No crash landing. The ship descended intact, east of the city. The . . . Terrestrials . . . were unharmed. Naturally, we feared them; they were strange to us. We had never before seen such beings."

"Stepped off the ship with guns blazing, did they?"

"Guns? No, no guns—"

"They raised their hands, didn't they, asked for help? You helped them; helped them to death."

"How could we know?" Fith moaned.

"How could you know a flotilla would show up in a few months looking for them, you mean? That was a shock, wasn't it? I'll bet you had a brisk time of it hiding the ship, and shutting everybody up. A close call, eh?"

"We were afraid," Shluh said. "We are a simple people. We feared the strange creatures from the alien craft. We did not kill them, but we felt it was as well that they . . . did not survive. Then, when the warships came, we realized our error, but we feared to speak. We purged our guilty leaders, concealed what had happened, and . . . offered our friendship. We invited the opening of diplomatic relations. We made a blunder, it is true, a great blunder. But we have tried to make amends . . ."

"Where is the ship?"

"The ship?"

"What did you do with it? It was too big to just walk off and forget. Where is it?"

The two Groacians exchanged looks.

"We wish to show our contrition," Fith said. "We will show you the ship."

"Miss Meuhl," Retief said. "If I don't come back in a reasonable length of time, transmit that recording to Sector Headquarters, sealed." He stood and looked at the Groaci.

"Let's go," he said.

Retief stooped under the heavy timbers shoring the entry to the cavern and peered into the gloom at the curving flank of the space-burned hull.

"Any lights in here?" he asked.

A Groacian threw a switch and a weak bluish glow sprang up. Retief walked along the raised wooden catwalk, studying the ship. Empty emplacements gaped below lenseless scanner eyes. Littered decking was visible within the half-open entry port. Near the bow the words 'IVS *Terrific*

B7 New Terra' were lettered in bright chrome duralloy.

"How did you get it in here?" Retief asked.

"It was hauled here from the landing point, some nine miles distant," Fith said, his voice thinner than ever. "This is a natural crevasse; the vessel was lowered into it and roofed over."

"How did you shield it so the detectors didn't pick it up?"

"All here is high-grade iron-ore," Fith said, waving a member. "Great veins of almost pure metal."

"Let's go inside."

Shluh came forward with a hand-lamp. The party entered the ship. Retief clambered up a narrow companionway and glanced around the interior of the control compartment. Dust was thick on the deck, the stanchions where acceleration couches had been mounted, the empty instrument panels, the litter of sheared bolts, and on scraps of wire and paper. A thin frosting of rust dulled the exposed metal where cutting torches had sliced away heavy shielding. There was a faint odor of stale bedding.

"The cargo compartment—" Shluh began.

"I've seen enough," Retief said. Silently, the Groacians led the way back out through the tunnel and into the late afternoon sunshine. As they climbed the slope to the steam car, Fith came to Retief's side.

"Indeed I hope that this will be the end of this unfortunate affair," he said. "Now that all has been fully and honestly shown."

"You can skip all that," Retief said. "You're nine years late. The crew was still alive when the Task Force called, I imagine. You killed them—or let them die—rather than take the chance of admitting what you'd done."

"We were at fault," Fith said abjectly. "Now we wish only friendship."

"The *Terrific* was a heavy cruiser, about twenty thousand tons." Retief looked grimly at the slender Foreign Officer official. "Where is she, Fith? I won't settle for a hundred-ton lifeboat."

Fith erected his eye stalks so violently that one eye-shield fell off.

"I know nothing of . . . of . . ." He stopped. His throat vibrated rapidly as he struggled for calm.

"My government can entertain no further accusations, Mr. Consul," he said at last. "I have been completely candid with you, I have overlooked your probing into matters not properly within your sphere of responsibility. My patience is at an end."

"Where is that ship?" Retief rapped out. "You never learn, do you? You're still convinced you can hide the whole thing and forget it. I'm telling you you can't."

"We return to the city now," Fith said. "I can do no more."

"You can and you will, Fith," Retief said. "I intend to get to the truth of this matter."

Fith spoke to Shluh in rapid Groacian. The police chief gestured to his four armed constables. They moved to ring Retief in.

Retief eyed Fith. "Don't try it" he said. "You'll just get yourself in deeper."

Fith clacked his mandibles angrily, his eye stalks canted aggressively toward the Terrestrial.

"Out of deference to your diplomatic status, Terrestrial, I shall ignore your insulting implications," Fith said in his reedy voice. "We will now return to the city."

Retief looked at the four policemen. "Sure," he said. "We'll cover the details later."

Fith followed him into the car and sat rigidly at the far end of the seat.

"I advise you to remain very close to your Consulate," Fith said. "I advise you to dismiss these fancies from your mind, and to enjoy the cultural aspects of life at Groac. Especially, I should not venture out of the city, or appear overly curious about matters of concern only to the Groacian government."

In the front seat, Shluh looked straight ahead. The loosely-sprung vehicle bobbed and swayed along the narrow highway. Retief listened to the rhythmic puffing of the motor and said nothing.

"Miss Meuhl," Retief said, "I want you to listen carefully to what I'm going to tell you. I have to move rapidly now, to catch the Groaci off guard."

"I'm sure I don't know what you're talking about," Miss Meuhl snapped, her eyes sharp behind the heavy lenses.

"If you'll listen, you may find out," Retief said. "I have no time to waste, Miss Meuhl. They won't be expecting an immediate move—I hope—and that may give me the latitude I need."

"You're still determined to make an issue of that incident," Miss Meuhl snorted. "I really can hardly blame the Groaci; they are not a sophisticated race; they had never before met aliens."

"You're ready to forgive a great deal, Miss Meuhl. But it's not what happened nine years ago I'm concerned with. It's what's happening now. I've told you that it was only a lifeboat the Groaci have hidden out. Don't you understand the implication? That vessel couldn't have come far; the cruiser itself must be somewhere nearby. I want to know where."

"The Groaci don't know. They're a very cultured, gentle people. You can do irreparable harm to the Terrestrial image if you insist—"

"We're wasting time," Retief said, as he crossed the room to his desk, opened a drawer, and took out a slim-barreled needler.

"This office is being watched; not very efficiently, if I know the Groaci. I think I can get past them all right."

"Where are you going with . . . that?" Miss Meuhl stared at the needler. "What in the world—"

"The Groaci won't waste any time destroying every piece of paper in their files relating to this affair. I have to get what I need before it's too late. If I wait for an official Enquiry Commission, they'll find nothing but blank smiles."

"You're out of your mind!" Miss Meuhl stood up, quivering with indignation. "You're like a . . . a . . ."

"You and I are in a tight spot, Miss Meuhl. The logical next move for the Groaci is to dispose of both of us. We're the only ones who know what happened. Fith almost did the job this afternoon, but I bluffed him out—for the moment."

Miss Meuhl emitted a shrill laugh. "Your fantasies are getting the better of you," she gasped. "In danger, indeed. Disposing of me! I've never heard anything so ridiculous."

"Stay in this office. Close and safe-lock the door. You've got food and water in the dispenser. I suggest you stock up, before they shut the supply down. Don't let anyone in, on any pretext whatever. I'll keep in touch with you via handphone."

"What are you planning to do?"

"If I don't make it back here, transmit the sealed record of this afternoon's conversation, along with the information I've given you. Beam it through on a Mayday priority. Then tell the Groaci what you've done and sit tight. I think you'll be all right. It won't be easy to blast in here and anyway, they won't make things worse by killing you in an obvious way. A Force can be here in a week."

"I'll do nothing of the sort! The Groaci are very fond of me! You . . . Johnny-come-lately! Roughneck! Setting out to destroy—"

"Blame it on me if it will make you feel any better," Retief said, "but don't be fool enough to trust them." He pulled on a cape, and opened the door.

"I'll be back in a couple of hours," he said. Miss Meuhl stared after him silently as he closed the door.

It was an hour before dawn when Retief keyed the combination to the safe-lock and stepped into the darkened Consular office. Miss Meuhl, dozing in a chair, awoke with a start. She looked at Retief, rose, snapped on a light, and turned to stare.

"What in the world— Where have you been? What's happened to your clothing?"

"I got a little dirty—don't worry about it." Retief went to his desk, opened a drawer, and replaced the needler.

"Where have you been?" Miss Meuhl demanded. "I stayed here."

"I'm glad you did," Retief said. "I hope you piled up a supply of food and water from the dispenser, too. We'll be holed up here for a week, at least." He jotted figures on a pad. "Warm up the official sender. I have a long transmission for Sector Headquarters."

"Are you going to tell me where you've been?"

"I have a message to get off first, Miss Meuhl," Retief said sharply. "I've been to the Foreign Ministry," he added. "I'll tell you all about it later."

"At this hour? There's no one there."

"Exactly."

Miss Meuhl gasped. "You mean you broke in? You burgled the Foreign Office?"

"That's right," Retief said calmly. "Now—"

"This is absolutely the end," Miss Meuhl said. "Thank heaven I've already—"

"Get that sender going, woman! This is important."

"I've already done so, Mr. Retief!" Miss Meuhl said harshly. "I've been waiting for you to come back here." She turned to the communicator and flipped levers. The screen snapped aglow, and a wavering long-distance image appeared.

"He's here now," Miss Muehl said to the screen. She looked at Retief triumphantly.

"That's good," said Retief. "I don't think the Groaci can knock us off the air, but—"

"I have done my duty, Mr. Retief; I made a full report of your activities to Sector Headquarters last night, as soon as you left this office. Any doubts I may have had as to the rightness of my decision have been completely dispelled by what you've just told me."

Retief looked at her levelly. "You've been a

busy girl, Miss Meuhl. Did you mention the six Terrestrials who were killed here?"

"That had no bearing on the matter of your wild behavior. I must say, in all my years in the Corps, I've never encountered a personality less suited to diplomatic work."

The screen crackled, the ten-second transmission lag having elapsed. "Mr. Retief," the face on the screen said sternly, "I am Counselor Nitworth, DSO-1, Deputy Under-Secretary for the Sector. I have received a report on your conduct which makes it mandatory for me to relieve you administratively. Pending the findings of a Board of Inquiry, you will—"

Retief reached out and snapped off the communicator. The triumphant look faded from Miss Meuhl's face.

"Why, what is the meaning—"

"If I'd listened any longer, I might have heard something I couldn't ignore. I can't afford that, at this moment. Listen, Miss Meuhl," Retief went on earnestly, "I've found the missing cruiser. It's—"

"You heard him relieve you!"

"I heard him say he was going to, Miss Meuhl. But until I've heard and acknowledged a verbal order, it has no force. If I'm wrong, he'll get my resignation. If I'm right, that suspension would be embarrassing all around."

"You're defying lawful authority. I'm in charge here now." Miss Meuhl stepped to the local communicator.

"I'm going to report this terrible thing to the Groaci at once, and offer my profound—"

"Don't touch that screen," Retief said. "You go sit in that corner where I can keep an eye on you.

I'm going to make a sealed tape for transmission to Headquarters, along with a call for an armed Task Force. Then we'll settle down to wait."

Retief, ignoring Miss Meuhl's fury, spoke into the recorder.

The local communicator chimed. Miss Meuhl jumped up and stared at it.

"Go ahead," Retief said. "Answer it."

A Groacian official appeared on the screen.

"Yolanda Meuhl," he said without preamble, "for the Foreign Minister of the Groacian Autonomy, I herewith accredit you as Terrestrial Consul to Groac, in accordance with the advices transmitted to my Government direct from the Terrestrial Headquarters. As Consul, you are requested to make available for questioning Mr. J. Retief, former Consul, in connection with the assault on two Peace Keepers, and illegal entry into the offices of the Ministry of Foreign Affairs."

"Why . . . why," Miss Meuhl stammered. "Yes, of course, and I do want to express my deepest regrets—"

Retief rose, went to the communicator, and assisted Miss Meuhl aside.

"Listen carefully, Fith," he said. "Your bluff has been called. You don't come in and we don't come out. Your camouflage worked for nine years, but it's all over now. I suggest you keep your heads and resist the temptation to make matters worse."

"Miss Meuhl," Fith replied, "a Peace Squad waits outside your Consulate. It is clear you are in the hands of a dangerous lunatic. As always, the Groaci wish only friendship with the Terrestrials, but—"

"Don't bother," Retief cut in. "You know what was in those files I looked over this morning."

Retief turned at a sound behind him. Miss Meuhl was at the door reaching for the safe-lock release.

"Don't!" Retief jumped . . . too late. The door burst inward, a crowd of crested Groaci pressed into the room, pushing Miss Meuhl back, and aimed scatter guns at Retief. Police Chief Shluh pushed forward.

"Attempt no violence, Terrestrial," he said. "I cannot promise to restrain my men."

"You're violating Terrestrial territory, Shluh," Retief said steadily. "I suggest you move back out the same way you came in."

"I invited them here," Miss Meuhl spoke up. "They are here at my express wish."

"Are they? Are you sure you meant to go this far, Miss Meuhl? A squad of armed Groaci in the Consulate?"

"You are the Consul, Miss Yolanda Meuhl," Shluh said. "Would it not be best if we removed this deranged person to a place of safety?"

"Yes," Miss Meuhl said. "You're quite right, Mr. Shluh. Please escort Mr. Retief to his quarters in this building."

"I don't advise you to violate my diplomatic immunity, Fith," Retief said.

"As Chief of Mission," Miss Meuhl said quickly, "I hereby waive immunity in the case of Mr. Retief."

Shluh produced a hand recorder. "Kindly repeat your statement, madame, officially," he said. "I wish no question—"

"Don't be a fool, woman," Retief said. "Don't you see what you're letting yourself in for? This would be a hell of a good time for you to figure out whose side you're on."

"I'm on the side of common decency!"

"You've been taken in. These people are concealing—"

"You think all women are fools, don't you, Mr. Retief?" She turned to the police chief and spoke into the microphone he held up.

"That's an illegal waiver," Retief said. "I'm Consul here, whatever rumors you've heard. This thing's coming out into the open, in spite of anything you can do; don't add violation of the Consulate to the list of Groacian atrocities."

"Take the man," Shluh said. Two tall Groaci came to Retief's side, guns aimed at his chest.

"Determined to hang yourselves, aren't you?" Retief said. "I hope you have sense enough not to lay a hand on this poor fool here." He jerked a thumb at Miss Meuhl. "She doesn't know anything. I hadn't had time to tell her yet. She thinks you're a band of angels."

The cop at Retief's side swung the butt of his scatter gun and connected solidly with Retief's jaw. Retief staggered against a Groacian, was caught and thrust upright, blood running down onto his shirt. Miss Meuhl yelped. Shluh barked at the guard in shrill Groacian, then turned to stare at Miss Meuhl.

"What has this man told you?"

"I—nothing. I refused to listen to his ravings."

"He said nothing to you of . . . some alleged . . . involvement."

"I've told you," Miss Muehl said sharply. She looked at the expressionless Groaci, then back at the blood on Retief's shirt.

"He told me nothing," she whispered. "I swear it."

"Let it lie, boys," Retief said, "before you spoil that good impression."

Shluh looked at Miss Meuhl for a long moment. Then he turned.

"Let us go," he said. He turned back to Miss Meuhl. "Do not leave this building until further advice."

"But . . . I am the Terrestrial Consul."

"For your safety, madam. The people are aroused at the beating of Groacian nationals by an . . . alien."

"So long, Meuhlsie," Retief said. "You played it real foxy."

"You'll . . . lock him in his quarters?" Miss Meuhl said.

"What is done with him now is a Groacian affair, Miss Meuhl. You yourself have withdrawn the protection of your government."

"I didn't mean—"

"Don't start having second thoughts," Retief said. "They can make you miserable."

"I had no choice. I had to consider the best interest of the Service."

"My mistake, I guess. I was thinking of the best interests of a Terrestrial cruiser with three hundred men aboard."

"Enough," Shluh said. "Remove this criminal." He gestured to the Peace Keepers.

"Move along," he said to Retief. He turned to Miss Meuhl.

"A pleasure to deal with you, Madam."

* * *

The police car started up and rolled away. The Peace Keeper in the front seat turned to look at Retief.

"To have some sport with it, and then to kill it," he said.

"To have a fair trial first," Shluh said. The car rocked and jounced, rounded a corner, and puffed along between ornamented pastel facades.

"To have a trial and then to have a bit of sport," the Peace Keeper said.

"To suck the eggs in your own hill," Retief said. "To make another stupid mistake."

Shluh raised his short ceremonial club and cracked Retief across the head. Retief shook his head, tensed—

The Peace Keeper in the front seat beside the driver turned and rammed the barrel of his scatter gun against Retief's ribs.

"To make no move, outworlder," he said. Shluh raised his club and carefully struck Retief again. He slumped.

The car, swaying, rounded another corner. Retief slid over against the police chief.

"To fend this animal—" Shluh began. His weak voice was cut off short as Retief's hand shot out, took him by the throat, and snapped him down onto the floor. As the guard on Retief's left lunged, Retief uppercut him, slamming his head against the door post. Retief grabbed the guard's scatter gun as it fell, and pushed it into the mandibles of the Groacian in the front seat.

"To put your pop-gun over the seat—carefully—and drop it," he said.

The driver slammed on his brakes, then whirled

to raise his gun. Retief cracked a gun barrel against the head of the Groacian.

"To keep your eye-stalks on the road," he said. The driver grabbed at the tiller and shrank against the window, watching Retief with one eye, driving with another.

"To gun this thing," Retief said. "To keep moving."

Shluh stirred on the floor. Retief put a foot on him, pressing him back. The Peace Keeper beside Retief moved. Retief pushed him off the seat onto the floor. He held the scatter gun with one hand and mopped at the blood on his face with the other. The car bounded over the irregular surface of the road, puffing furiously.

"Your death will not be an easy one, Terrestrial," Shluh said to Terran.

"No easier than I can help," Retief said. "Shut up for now. I want to think."

The car, passing the last of the relief-encrusted mounds, sped along between tilled fields.

"Slow down," Retief said. The driver obeyed.

"Turn down this side road."

The car bumped off onto an unpaved surface, then threaded its way back among tall stalks.

"Stop here." The car stopped, blew off steam, and sat trembling as the hot engine idled.

Retief opened the door, taking his foot off Shluh.

"Sit up," he ordered. "You two in front listen carefully." Shluh sat up, rubbing his throat.

"Three of you are getting out here. Good old Shluh is going to stick around to drive for me. If I get that nervous feeling that you're after me, I'll toss him out. That will be pretty messy, at high speed. Shluh, tell them to sit tight until dark and forget about sounding any alarms. I'd hate to see you split open and spill all over the pavement."

"To burst your throat sac, evil-smelling beast!" Shluh hissed in Groacian.

"Sorry, I haven't got one." Retief put the gun under Shluh's ear. "Tell them, Shluh; I can drive myself, in a pinch."

"To do as the foreign one says; to stay hidden until dark," Shluh said.

"Everybody out," Retief said. "And take this with you." He nudged the unconscious Groacian. "Shluh, you get in the driver's seat. You others stay where I can see you."

Retief watched as the Groaci silently followed instructions.

"All right, Shluh," Retief said softly. "Let's go. Take me to Groac Spaceport by the shortest route that doesn't go through the city, and be very careful about making any sudden movements."

Forty minutes later Shluh steered the car up to the sentry-guarded gate in the security fence surrounding the military enclosure at Groac Spaceport.

"Don't yield to any rash impulses," Retief whispered as a crested Groacian soldier came up. Shluh grated his mandibles in helpless fury.

"Drone-master Shluh, Internal Security," he croaked. The guard tilted his eyes toward Retief.

"The guest of the Autonomy," Shluh added. "To let me pass or to rot in this spot, fool?"

"To pass, Drone-master," the sentry mumbled. He was still staring at Retief as the car moved jerkily away.

"You are as good as pegged-out on the hill in the pleasure pits now, Terrestrial," Shluh said in Terran. "Why do you venture here?"

"Pull over there in the shadow of the tower and stop," Retief said.

Shluh complied. Retief studied a row of four slender ships silhouetted against the early dawn colors of the sky.

"Which of those boats are ready to lift?" Retief demanded.

Shluh swivelled a choleric eye.

"All of them are shuttles; they have no range. They will not help you."

"To answer the question, Shluh, or to get another crack on his head."

"You are not like other Terrestrials, you are a mad dog."

"We'll rough out a character sketch of me later. Are they fueled up? You know the procedures here. Did those shuttles just get in, or is that the ready line?"

"Yes. All are fueled and ready for take-off."

"I hope you're right, Shluh. You and I are going to drive over and get in one; if it doesn't lift, I'll kill you and try the next one. Let's go."

"You are mad. I have told you: these boats have not more than ten thousand ton-seconds capacity; they are useful only for satellite runs."

"Never mind the details. Let's try the first in line."

Shluh let in the clutch and the steam car clanked and heaved, rolling off toward the line of boats.

"Not the first in line," Shluh said suddenly. "The last is the most likely to be fueled. But—"

"Smart grasshopper," Retief said. "Pull up to the entry port, hop out, and go right up. I'll be right behind you."

"The gangway guard. The challenging of—"

"More details. Just give him a dirty look and say what's necessary. You know the technique."

The car passed under the stern of the first boat, then the second. There was no alarm. It rounded the third and shuddered to a stop by the open port of the last vessel.

"Out," Retief said. "To make it snappy."

Shluh stepped from the car, hesitated as the guard came to attention, then hissed at him and mounted the steps. The guard looked wonderingly at Retief, mandibles slack.

"An outworlder!" he said. He unlimbered his scatter gun. "To stop here, meat-faced one."

Up ahead, Shluh turned.

"To snap to attention, litter-mate of drones," Retief rasped in Groacian. The guard jumped, waved his eye stalks, and came to attention.

"About face!" Retief hissed. "To hell out of here—march!"

The guard tramped off across the ramp. Retief took the steps two at a time, slammed the port shut behind himself.

"I'm glad your boys have a little discipline, Shluh," Retief said. "What did you say to him?"

"I but—"

"Never mind. We're in. Get up to the control compartment."

"What do you know of Groacian Naval vessels?"

"Plenty. This is a straight copy from the life boat you lads hijacked. I can run it. Get going."

Retief followed Shluh up the companionway into the cramped control room.

"Tie in, Shluh," Retief ordered.

"This is insane. We have only fuel enough for a one-way transit to the satellite; we cannot enter orbit, nor can we land again! To lift this boat is death. Release me. I promise you immunity."

"If I have to tie you in myself, I might bend your head in the process."

Shluh crawled onto the couch, and strapped in.

"Give it up," he said. "I will see that you are re-instated—with honor. I will guarantee a safe-conduct—"

"Count-down," Retief said. He threw in the autopilot.

"It is death!" Shluh screeched.

The gyros hummed, timers ticked, relays closed. Retief lay relaxed on the acceleration pad. Shluh breathed noisily, his mandibles clicking rapidly.

"That I had fled in time," he said in a hoarse whisper. "This is not a good death."

"No death is a good death," Retief said, "not for a while yet." The red light flashed on in the center of the panel, and sound roared out into the breaking day. The ship trembled, then lifted. Retief could hear Shluh's whimpering even through the roar of the drive.

"Perihelion," Shluh said dully. "To begin now the long fall back."

"Not quite," Retief said. "I figure eighty-five seconds to go." He scanned the instruments, frowning.

"We will not reach the surface, of course," Shluh said, "the pips on the screen are missiles. We have a rendezvous in space, Retief. In your madness, may you be content."

"They're fifteen minutes behind us, Shluh. Your defenses are sluggish."

"Nevermore to burrow in the grey sands of Groac," Shluh mourned.

Retief's eyes were fixed on a dial face.

"Any time now," he said softly. Shluh canted his eye stalks.

"What do you seek?"

Retief stiffened. "Look at the screen," he said. Shluh looked. A glowing point, off-center, moving rapidly across the grid . . .

"What—?"

"Later—"

Shluh watched as Retief's eyes darted from one needle to another.

"How . . ."

"For your own neck's sake, Shluh, you'd better hope this works." He flipped the sending key.

"2396 TR-42 G, this is the Terrestrial Consul at Groac, aboard Groac 902, vectoring on you at an MP fix of 91/54/942. Can you read me? Over."

"What forlorn gesture is this?" Shluh whispered. "You cry in the night to emptiness."

"Button your mandibles," Retief snapped, listening. There was a faint hum of stellar background noise. Retief repeated his call.

"Maybe they hear but can't answer," he muttered. He flipped the key.

"2396, you've got forty seconds to lock a tractor beam on me, before I shoot past you."

"To call into the void," said Shluh. "To—"

"Look at the DV screen."

Shluh twisted his head and looked. Against the background mist of stars, a shape loomed, dark and inert.

"It is . . . a ship," he said, "a monster ship . . ."

"That's her," Retief said. "Nine years and a few

months out of New Terra on a routine mapping mission; the missing cruiser, *IVS Terrific*."

"Impossible," Shluh hissed. "The bulk swings in a deep cometary orbit."

"Right, and now it's making its close swing past Groac."

"You think to match orbits with the derelict? Without power? Our meeting will be a violent one, if that is your intent."

"We won't hit; we'll make our pass at about five thousand yards."

"To what end, Terrestrial? You have found your lost ship; what then? Is this glimpse worth the death we die?"

"Maybe they're not dead," Retief said.

"Not dead?" Shluh lapsed into Groacian. "To have died in the burrow of one's youth. To have burst my throat sac before I embarked with a mad alien to call up the dead."

"2396, make it snappy," Retief called. The speaker crackled heedlessly. The dark image on the screen drifted past, dwindling now.

"Nine years, and the mad one speaking as to friends," Shluh raved. "Nine years dead, and still to seek them."

"Another ten seconds," Retief said softly, "and we're out of range. Look alive, boys."

"Was this your plan, Retief?" Shluh reverted to Terran. "Did you flee Groac and risk all on this slender thread?"

"How long would I have lasted in a Groaci prison?"

"Long and long, my Retief," Shluh hissed, "under the blade of an artist."

Abruptly the ship trembled, seemed to drag,

rolling the two passengers in their couches. Shluh hissed as the restraining harness cut into him. The shuttle boat was pivoting heavily, up-ending. Crushing acceleration forces built. Shluh gasped, crying out shrilly.

"What . . . is . . . it . . . ?"

"It looks," said Retief, "like we've had a little bit of luck."

"On our second pass," the gaunt-faced officer said, "they let fly with something. I don't know how it got past our screens. It socked home in the stern and put the main pipe off the air. I threw full power to the emergency shields, and broadcast our identification on a scatter that should have hit every receiver within a parsec; nothing. Then the transmitter blew. I was a fool to send the boat down, but I couldn't believe, somehow . . ."

"In a way it's lucky you did, captain. That was my only lead."

"They tried to finish us after that. But, with full power to the screens, nothing they had could get through. Then they called on us to surrender."

Retief nodded. "I take it you weren't tempted?"

"More than you know. It was a long swing out on our first circuit. Then coming back in, we figured we'd hit. As a last resort I would have pulled back power from the screens and tried to adjust the orbit with the steering jets, but the bombardment was pretty heavy. I don't think we'd have made it. Then we swung past and headed out again. We've got a three-year period. Don't think I didn't consider throwing in the towel."

"Why didn't you?"

"The information we have is important. We've

got plenty of stores aboard, enough for another ten years, if necessary. Sooner or later I knew a Corps search vessel would find us."

Retief cleared his throat. "I'm glad you stuck with it, Captain. Even a backwater world like Groac can kill a lot of people when it runs amok."

"What I didn't know," the captain went on, "was that we're not in a stable orbit. We're going to graze atmosphere pretty deeply this pass, and in another sixty days we'd be back to stay. I guess the Groaci would be ready for us."

"No wonder they were sitting on this so tight. They were almost in the clear."

"And you're here now," the captain said. "Nine years, and we weren't forgotten. I knew we could count on—"

"It's over now, captain. That's what counts."

"Home . . . After nine years . . ."

"I'd like to take a look at the films you mentioned," Retief said. "The ones showing the installations on the satellite."

The captain complied. Retief watched as the scene unrolled, showing the bleak surface of the tiny moon as the *Terrific* had seen it, nine years before. In harsh black and white, row on row of identical hulls cast long shadows across the pitted metallic surface of the satellite.

"They had quite a little surprise planned; your visit must have panicked them," Retief said.

"They should be about ready to go, by now. Nine years . . ."

"Hold that picture," Retief said suddenly. "What's that ragged black line across the plain there?"

"I think it's a fissure. The crystalline structure—"

"I've got what may be an idea," Retief said. "I

had a look at some classified files last night, at the Foreign Office. One was a progress report on a fissionable stock-pile. It didn't make much sense at the time. Now I get the picture. Which is the north end of that crevasse?"

"At the top of the picture."

"Unless I'm badly mistaken, that's the bomb dump. The Groaci like to tuck things underground. I wonder what a direct hit with a 50 megaton missile would do to it?"

"If that's an ordnance storage dump," the captain said, "it's an experiment I'd like to try."

"Can you hit it?"

"I've got fifty heavy missiles aboard. If I fire them in direct-sequence, it should saturate the defenses. Yes, I can hit it."

"The range isn't too great?"

"These are the deluxe models." The captain smiled balefully. "Video guidance. We could steer them into a bar and park 'em on a stool."

"What do you say we try it?"

"I've been wanting a solid target for a long time," the captain said.

Half an hour later, Retief propelled Shluh into a seat before the screen.

"That expanding dust cloud used to be the satellite of Groac, Shluh," he said. "Looks like something happened to it."

The police chief stared at the picture.

"Too bad," Retief said. "But then it wasn't of any importance, was it, Shluh?"

Shluh muttered incomprehensibly.

*　　*　　*

"Just a bare hunk of iron, Shluh, as the Foreign Office assured me when I asked for information."

"I wish you'd keep your prisoner out of sight," the captain said. "I have a hard time keeping my hands off him."

"Shluh wants to help, captain. He's been a bad boy and I have a feeling he'd like to co-operate with us now, especially in view of the eminent arrival of a Terrestrial ship, and the dust cloud out there," Retief said.

"What do you mean?"

"Captain, you can ride it out for another week, contact the ship when it arrives, get a tow in, and your troubles are over. When your films are shown in the proper quarter, a Peace Force will come out here and reduce Groac to a sub-technical cultural level and set up a monitor system to insure she doesn't get any more expansionist ideas—not that she can do much now, with her handy iron mine in the sky gone."

"That's right, and—"

"On the other hand, there's what I might call the diplomatic approach . . ."

He explained at length. The captain looked at him thoughtfully.

"I'll go along," he said. "What about this fellow?"

Retief turned to Shluh. The Groacian shuddered, retracting his eye stalks.

"I will do it," he said faintly.

"Right," Retief said. "Captain, if you'll have your men bring in the transmitter from the shuttle, I'll place a call to a fellow named Fith at the Foreign Office." He turned to Shluh. "And when I get him, Shluh, you'll do everything exactly as I've told you—or have Terrestrial monitors dictating in Groac City."

"Quite candidly, Retief," Counselor Nitworth said, "I'm rather nonplussed. Mr. Fith of the Foreign Office seemed almost painfully lavish in your praise. He seems most eager to please you. In the light of some of the evidence I've turned up of highly irregular behavior on your part, it's difficult to understand."

"Fith and I have been through a lot together," Retief said. "We understand each other."

"You have no cause for complacency, Retief," Nitworth said. "Miss Meuhl was quite justified in reporting your case. Of course, had she known that you were assisting Mr. Fith in his marvelous work, she would have modified her report somewhat, no doubt. You should have confided in her."

"Fith wanted to keep it secret, in case it didn't work out. You know how it is."

"Of course. And as soon as Miss Meuhl recovers from her nervous breakdown, there'll be a nice promotion awaiting her. The girl more than deserves it for her years of unswerving devotion to Corps policy."

"Unswerving," Retief said. "I'll go along with that."

"As well you may, Retief. You've not acquitted yourself well in this assignment. I'm arranging for a transfer; you've alienated too many of the local people."

"But as you said, Fith speaks highly of me . . ."

"True. It's the cultural intelligentsia I'm referring to. Miss Meuhl's records show that you deliberately affronted a number of influential groups by boycotting—"

"Tone deaf," Retief said. "To me a Groacian blowing a nose-whistle sounds like a Groacian blowing a nose-whistle."

"You have to come to terms with local aesthetic values. Learn to know the people as they really are. It's apparent from some of the remarks Miss Meuhl quoted in her report that you held the Groaci in rather low esteem. But how wrong you were. All the while they were working unceasingly to rescue those brave lads marooned aboard our cruiser. They pressed on, even after we ourselves had abandoned the search. And when they discovered that it had been a collision with their satellite which disabled the craft, they made that magnificent gesture—unprecedented. One hundred thousand credits in gold to each crew member, as a token of Groacian sympathy."

"A handsome gesture," Retief murmured.

"I hope, Retief, that you've learned from this incident. In view of the helpful part you played in advising Mr. Fith in matters of procedure to assist in his search, I'm not recommending a reduction in grade. We'll overlook the affair, give you a clean slate. But in the future, I'll be watching you closely."

"You can't win 'em all," Retief said.

"You'd better pack up; you'll be coming along with us in the morning." Nitworth shuffled his papers together. "I'm sorry that I can't file a more flattering report on you. I would have liked to recommend your promotion, along with Miss Meuhl's."

"That's okay," Retief said. "I have my memories."

Palace
Revolution

. . . Ofttimes, the expertese displayed by experienced Terrestrial Chiefs of Mission in the analysis of local political currents enabled these dedicated senior officers to secure acceptance of Corps commercial programs under seemingly insurmountable conditions of adversity. Ambassador Crodfoller's virtuoso performance in the reconciliation of rival elements at Petreac added new lustre to Corps prestige . . .

Vol VIII, reel 8. 489 A. E. (AD 2950)

RETIEF PAUSED before a tall mirror to check the overlap of the four sets of lapels that ornamented the vermilion cut-away of a First Secretary and Consul.

"Come along, Retief," Magnan said. "The ambassador has a word to say to the staff before we go in."

"I hope he isn't going to change the spontaneous speech he plans to make when the Potentate impulsively suggests a trade agreement along the lines they've been discussing for the last two months."

"Your derisive attitude is uncalled for, Retief," Magnan said sharply. "I think you realize it's delayed your promotion in the Corps."

Retief took a last glance in the mirror. "I'm not sure I want a promotion. It would mean more lapels."

Ambassador Crodfoller pursed his lips, waiting

152

until Retief and Magnan took places in the ring of Terrestrial diplomats around him.

"A word of caution only, gentlemen. Keep always foremost in your minds the necessity for our identification with the Nenni Caste. Even a hint of familiarity with lower echelons could mean the failure of the mission. Let us remember: the Nenni represent authority here on Petreac; their traditions must be observed, whatever our personal preferences. Let's go along now; the Potentate will be making his entrance any moment."

Magnan came to Retief's side as they moved toward the salon.

"The ambassador's remarks were addressed chiefly to you, Retief," he said. "Your laxness in these matters is notorious. Naturally, I believe firmly in democratic principles myself."

"Have you ever had a feeling, Mr. Magnan, that there's a lot going on here that we don't know about?"

Magnan nodded. "Quite so; Ambassador Crodfoller's point exactly. Matters which are not of concern to the Nenni are of no concern to us."

"Another feeling I get is that the Nenni aren't very bright. Now suppose—"

"I'm not given to suppositions, Retief. We're here to implement the policies of the Chief of Mission. And I should dislike to be in the shoes of a member of the Staff whose conduct jeopardized the agreement that's to be concluded here tonight."

A bearer with a tray of drinks rounded a fluted column, shied as he confronted the diplomats, fumbled the tray, grabbed, and sent a glass crashing to the floor. Magnan leaped back, slapping at the purple cloth of his pants leg. Retief's hand shot out and steadied the tray. The servant rolled his terrified eyes.

"I'll take one of those, now that you're here," Retief said easily, lifting a glass from the tray. "No harm done. Mr. Magnan's just warming up for the big dance."

A Nenni major-domo bustled up, rubbing his hands politely.

"Some trouble here? What happened, Honorables, what, what . . ."

"The blundering idiot," Magnan spluttered. "How dare—"

"You're quite an actor, Mr. Magnan," Retief said. "If I didn't know about your democratic principles, I'd think you were really angry."

The servant ducked his head and scuttled away.

"Has this fellow given dissatisfaction . . . ?" The major-domo eyed the retreating bearer.

"I dropped my glass," Retief said. "Mr. Magnan's upset because he hates to see liquor wasted."

Retief turned and found himself face-to-face with Ambassador Crodfoller.

"I witnessed that," the ambassador hissed. "By the goodness of Providence the Potentate and his retinue haven't appeared yet, but I can assure you the servants saw it. A more un-Nenni-like display I would find it difficult to imagine."

Retief arranged his features in an expression of deep interest. "More un-Nenni-like, sir? I'm not sure I—"

"Bah!" The ambassador glared at Retief. "Your reputation has preceded you, sir. Your name is associated with a number of the most bizarre incidents in Corps history. I'm warning you; I'll tolerate nothing." He turned and stalked away.

"Ambassador-baiting is a dangerous sport, Retief," Magnan said.

Retief took a swallow of his drink. "Still, it's better than no sport at all."

"Your time would be better spent observing the Nenni mannerisms; frankly, Retief, you're not fitting into the group at all well."

"I'll be candid with you, Mr. Magnan; the group gives me the willies."

"Oh, the Nenni are a trifle frivolous, I'll concede. But it's with them that we must deal. And you'd be making a contribution to the overall mission if you abandoned that rather arrogant manner of yours." Magnan looked at Retief critically. "You can't help your height, of course, but couldn't you curve your back just a bit—and possibly assume a more placating expression? Just act a little more . . ."

"Girlish?"

"Exactly." Magnan nodded, then looked sharply at Retief.

Retief drained his glass and put it on a passing tray.

"I'm better at acting girlish when I'm well juiced," he said. "But I can't face another sorghum and soda. I suppose it would be un-Nenni-like to slip one of the servants a credit and ask for a Scotch and water."

"Decidedly." Magnan glanced toward a sound across the room.

"Ah, here's the Potentate now . . ." He hurried off.

Retief watched the bearers coming and going, bringing trays laden with drinks, carrying off empties. There was a lull in the drinking now, as the diplomats gathered around the periwigged chief of state and his courtiers. Bearers loitered near the service door, eyeing the notables. Retief strolled over to the service door and pushed through it into a narrow white-tiled hall filled with kitchen odors. Silent servants gaped as he passed and watched him as he moved along to the kitchen door and stepped inside.

A dozen or more low-caste Petreacans, gathered around a long table in the center of the room, looked up, startled. A heap of long-bladed bread knives, carving knives and cleavers lay in the center of the table. Other knives were thrust into belts or held in the hands of the men. A fat man in the yellow sarong of a cook stood frozen in the act of handing a twelve-inch cheese-knife to a tall one-eyed sweeper.

Retief took one glance, then let his eyes wander to a far corner of the room. Humming a careless little tune, he sauntered across to the open liquor shelves, selected a garish green bottle, then turned unhurriedly back toward the door. The group of servants watched him, transfixed.

As Retief reached the door, it swung inward. Magnan stood in the doorway, looking at him.

"I had a premonition," he said.

"I'll bet it was a dandy. You must tell me all about it—in the salon."

"We'll have this out right here," Magnan snapped. "I've warned you—" His voice trailed off as he took in the scene around the table.

"After you," Retief said, nudging Magnan toward the door.

"What's going on here?" Magnan barked. He stared at the men and started around Retief. A hand stopped him.

"Let's be going," Retief said, propelling Magnan toward the hall.

"Those knives!" Magnan yelped. "Take your hands off me, Retief! What are you men—"

Retief glanced back. The fat cook gestured suddenly, and the men faded back. The cook stood, arm cocked, a knife across his palm.

"Close the door and make no sound," he said softly.

Magnan pressed back against Retief. "Let's . . . r-run . . ." he faltered.

Retief turned slowly, put his hands up.

"I don't run very well with a knife in my back," he said. "Stand very still, Mr. Magnan, and do just what he tells you."

"Take them out through the back," the cook said.

"What does he mean," Magnan spluttered. "Here, you—"

"Silence," the cook said, almost casually. Magnan gaped at him, then closed his mouth.

Two of the men with knives came to Retief's side, gestured, grinning broadly.

"Let's go, peacocks," said one.

Retief and Magnan silently crossed the kitchen, went out the back door, stopped on command, and stood waiting. The sky was brilliant with stars and a gentle breeze stirred the tree-tops beyond the garden. Behind them the servants talked in low voices.

"You go too, Illy," the cook was saying.

"Do it here," said another.

"And carry them down?"

"Pitch 'em behind the hedge."

"I said the river. Three of you is plenty for a couple of Nenni dandies."

"They're foreigners, not Nenni. We don't know—"

"So they're foreign Nenni. Makes no difference. I've seen them. I need every man here; now get going."

"What about the big guy?"

"Him? He waltzed into the room and didn't notice a thing. But watch the other one."

At a prod from a knife point, Retief moved off down the walk, two of the escort behind him and Magnan, another going ahead to scout the way.

Magnan moved closer to Retief.

"Say," he said in a whisper, "that fellow in the lead—isn't he the one who spilled the drink? The one you took the blame for?"

"That's him, all right. He doesn't seem nervous anymore, I notice."

"You saved him from serious punishment," Magnan said. "He'll be grateful; he'll let us go. . . ."

"Better check with the fellows with the knives before you act on that."

"Say something to him," Magnan hissed, "remind him."

The lead man fell back in line with Retief and Magnan.

"These two are scared of you," he said, grinning and jerking a thumb toward the knife-handlers. "They haven't worked round the Nenni like me; they don't know you."

"Don't you recognize this gentleman?" Magnan said. "He's—"

"He did me a favor," the man said. "I remember."

"What's it all about?" Retief said.

"The revolution. We're taking over now."

"Who's 'we'?"

"The People's Anti-Fascist Freedom League."

"What are all the knives for?"

"For the Nenni; and for you foreigners."

"What do you mean?" gasped Magnan.

"We'll slit all the throats at one time; saves a lot of running around."

"When will that be?"

"Just at dawn—and dawn comes early, this time of year. By full daylight the PAFFL will be in charge."

"You'll never succeed," Magnan said. "A few servants with knives; you'll all be caught and executed."

"By who; the Nenni?" The man laughed. "You Nenni are a caution."

"But we're not Nenni—"

"We've watched you; you're the same. You're part of the same blood-sucking class."

"There are better ways," Magnan said. "This killing won't help you. I'll personally see to it that your grievances are heard in the Corps Courts. I can assure you that the plight of the down-trodden workers will be alleviated. Equal rights for all."

"Threats won't help you," the man said. "You don't scare me."

"Threats? I'm promising relief to the exploited classes of Petreac."

"You must be nuts. You trying to upset the system or something?"

"Isn't that the purpose of your revolution?"

"Look, Nenni, we're tired of you Nenni getting all the graft. We want our turn. What good it do us to run Petreac if there's no loot?"

"You mean you intend to oppress the people? But they're your own group."

"Group, schmoop. We're taking all the chances; we're doing the work. We deserve the pay-off. You think we're throwing up good jobs for the fun of it?"

"You're basing a revolt on these cynical premises?"

"Wise up, Nenni; there's never been a revolution for any other reason."

"Who's in charge of this?" Retief said.

"Shoke, the head chef."

"I mean the big boss; who tells Shoke what to do?"

"Oh, that's Zorn. Look out, here's where we start down the slope. It's slippery."

"Look," Magnan said. "You. This—"

"My name's Illy."

"Mr. Illy, this man showed you mercy when he could have had you beaten."

"Keep moving. Yeah, I said I was grateful."

"Yes," Magnan said, swallowing hard. "A noble emotion, gratitude."

"I always try to pay back a good turn," Illy said. "Watch your step now on this sea-wall."

"You'll never regret it."

"This is far enough." Illy motioned to one of the knife men. "Give me your knife, Vug."

The man passed his knife to Illy. There was an odor of sea-mud and kelp. Small waves slapped against the stones of the sea-wall. The wind was stronger here.

"I know a neat stroke," Illy said. "Practically painless. Who's first?"

"What do you mean?" Magnan quavered.

"I said I was grateful; I'll do it myself, give you a

a nice clean job. You know these amateurs: botch it up and have a guy floppin' around, yellin' and spatterin' everybody up."

"I'm first," Retief said. He pushed past Magnan, stopped suddenly, and drove a straight punch at Illy's mouth.

The long blade flicked harmlessly over Retief's shoulder as Illy fell. Retief took the unarmed servant by the throat and belt, lifted him, and slammed him against the third man. Both screamed as they tumbled from the sea-wall into the water with a mighty splash. Retief turned back to Illy, pulled off the man's belt, and strapped his hands together.

Magnan found his voice. "You . . . we . . . they . . ."

"I know."

"We've got to get back," Magnan said. "Warn them."

"We'd never get through the rebel cordon around the palace. And if we did, trying to give an alarm would only set the assassinations off early."

"We can't just . . ."

"We've got to go to the source: this fellow Zorn. Get him to call it off."

"We'd be killed. At least we're safe here."

Illy groaned and opened his eyes. He sat up.

"On your feet, Illy," Retief said.

Illy looked around. "I'm sick."

"The damp air is bad for you. Let's be going." Retief pulled the man to his feet. "Where does Zorn stay when he's in town?"

"What happened? Where's Vug and . . ."

"They had an accident. Fell in the pond."

Illy gazed down at the restless black water.

"I guess I had you Nenni figured wrong."

"We Nenni have hidden qualities. Let's get moving before Vug and Slug make it to shore and start it all over again."

"No hurry," Illy said. "They can't swim." He spat into the water. "So long, Vug. So long, Toscin. Take a pull at the Hell Horn for me." He started off along the sea wall toward the sound of the surf.

"You want to see Zorn, I'll take you to see Zorn. I can't swim either."

"I take it," Retief said, "that the casino is a front for his political activities."

"He makes plenty off it. This PAFFL is a new kick. I never heard about it until maybe a couple months ago."

Retief motioned toward a dark shed with an open door.

"We'll stop here," he said, "long enough to strip the gadgets off these uniforms."

Illy, hands strapped behind his back, stood by and watched as Retief and Magnan removed medals, ribbons, orders, and insignia from the formal diplomatic garments.

"This may help some," Retief said, "if the word is out that two diplomats are loose."

"It's a breeze," Illy said. "We see cats in purple and orange tailcoats all the time."

"I hope you're right," Retief said. "But if we're called, you'll be the first to go, Illy."

"You're a funny kind of Nenni," Illy said, eyeing Retief. "Toscin and Vug must be wonderin' what happened to 'em."

"If you think I'm good at drowning people, you ought to see me with a knife. Let's get going."

"It's only a little way now. But you better

untie me. Somebody's liable to notice it and start askin' questions and get me killed."

"I'll take the chance. How do we get to the casino?"

"We follow this street. When we get to the Drunkard's Stairs we go up and it's right in front of us. A pink front with a sign like a big luck wheel."

"Give me your belt, Magnan," Retief said.

Magnan handed it over.

"Lie down, Illy."

The servant looked at Retief.

"Vug and Toscin will be glad to see me. But they'll never believe me." He lay down. Retief strapped his feet together and stuffed a handkerchief in his mouth.

"Why are you doing that?" Magnan asked. "We need him."

"We know the way now and we don't need anyone to announce our arrival."

Magnan looked at the man. "Maybe you'd better— ah, cut his throat."

Illy rolled his eyes.

"That's a very un-Nenni-like suggestion, Mr. Magnan," Retief said. "But if we have any trouble finding the casino following his directions, I'll give it serious thought."

There were few people in the narrow street. Shops were shuttered, windows dark.

"Maybe they heard about the coup," Magnan said. "They're lying low."

"More likely they're at the palace checking out knives."

They rounded a corner, stepped over a man curled in the gutter snoring heavily, and found themselves at the foot of a long flight of littered stone steps.

"The Drunkard's Stairs are plainly marked," Magnan sniffed.

"I hear sounds up there . . . sounds of merry-making."

"Maybe we'd better go back."

"Merrymaking doesn't scare me. Come to think of it, I don't know what the word means." Retief started up, Magnan behind him.

At the top of the long stair a dense throng milled in the alley-like street.

A giant illuminated roulette wheel revolved slowly above them. A loud-speaker blared the chant of the croupiers from the tables inside. Magnan and Retief moved through the crowd toward the wide-open doors.

Magnan plucked at Retief's sleeve. "Are you sure we ought to push right in like this? Maybe we ought to wait a bit, look around."

"When you're where you have no business being," Retief said, "always stride along purpose-fully. If you loiter, people begin to get curious."

Inside, a mob packed the wide low-ceilinged room and clustered around gambling devices in the form of towers, tables, and basins.

"What do we do now?" Magnan asked.

"We gamble. How much money do you have in your pockets?"

"Why . . . a few credits . . ." Magnan handed the money to Retief. "But what about the man Zorn?"

"A purple cutaway is conspicuous enough, without ignoring the tables. We'll get to Zorn in due course."

"Your pleasure, gents," a bullet-headed man said, eyeing the colorful evening clothes of the diplomats. "You'll be wantin' to try your luck at the Zoop tower, I'd guess. A game for real sporting gents."

"Why . . . ah . . ." Magnan said.

"What's a Zoop tower?" Retief asked.

"Out-of-towners, hey?" The bullet-headed man shifted his dope-stick to the other corner of his mouth. "Zoop is a great a little game. Two teams of players buy into the pot; each player takes a lever; the object is to make the ball drop from the top of the tower into your net. Okay?"

"What's the ante?"

"I got a hundred-credit pot workin' now, gents."

Retief nodded. "We'll try it."

The shill led the way to an eight-foot tower mounted on gimbals. Two perspiring men in the trade-class pullovers gripped two of the levers that controlled the tilt of the tower. A white ball lay in a hollow in the thick glass platform at the top. From the center an intricate pattern of grooves led out to the edge of the glass. Retief and Magnan took chairs before the two free levers.

"When the light goes on, gents, work the lever to jack the tower. You got three gears; takes a good arm to work top gear. That's this button here. The little little knob controls what way you're goin'. May the best team win. I'll take the hundred credits now."

Retief handed over the money. A red light flashed on, and Retief tried the elevator. It moved easily, with a ratcheting sound. The tower trembled, slowly tilted toward the two perspiring workmen pumping frantically at their levers. Magnan started slowly, accelerating as he saw the direction the tower was taking.

"Faster, Retief," he said. "They're winning."

"This is against the clock, gents," the bullet-headed man said. "If nobody wins when the light goes off, the house takes all."

"Crank it over to the left," Retief said.

"I'm getting tired."

"Shift to a lower gear."

The tower leaned. The ball stirred and rolled into a concentric channel. Retief shifted to middle gear and worked the lever. The tower, creaking to a stop, started back upright.

"There isn't any lower gear," Magnan gasped. One of the two on the other side of the tower shifted to middle gear; the other followed suit. They worked harder now, heaving against the stiff levers. The tower quivered, then moved slowly toward their side.

"I'm exhausted," Magnan gasped. Dropping the lever, he lolled back in the chair, gulping air. Retief, shifting position, took Magnan's lever with his left hand.

"Shift it to middle gear," he said. Magnan gulped, punched the button and slumped back, panting.

"My arm," he said. "I've injured myself."

The two men in pullovers conferred hurriedly as they cranked their levers; then one punched a button, and the other reached across, using his left arm to help.

"They've shifted to high," Magnan said. "Give up, it's hopeless."

"Shift me to high. Both buttons."

Magnan complied. Retief's shoulders bulged. He brought one lever down, then the other, alternately, slowly at first, then faster. The tower jerked, tilted toward him, farther. . . . The ball rolled in the channel, found an outlet—

Abruptly, both Retief's levers froze. The tower trembled, wavered, and moved back. Retief heaved. One lever folded at the base, bent down, and snapped off short. Retief braced his feet, gripped the other lever with both hands and pulled. There was a squeal of metal, a loud twang. The lever came free, a length of broken cable flopping into view. The tower fell over as the two on the other side scrambled aside.

"Hey!" the croupier yelled, appearing from the crowd. "You wrecked my equipment!"

Retief got up and faced him.

"Does Zorn know you've got your tower rigged for suckers?"

"You tryin' to call me a cheat?"

The crowd had fallen back, ringing the two men. The croupier glanced around. With a lightning motion he pulled out a knife.

"That'll be five hundred credits for the equipment," he said. "Nobody calls Kippy a cheat."

Retief picked up the broken lever.

"Don't make me hit you with this, Kippy."

Kippy looked at the bar.

"Comin' in here," he said indignantly, looking to the crowd for support, "bustin' up my rig, threatenin' me . . ."

"I want a hundred credits," Retief said. "Now."

"Highway robbery!" Kippy yelled.

"Better pay up," somebody said.

"Hit him, mister," another in the crowd yelled.

A broad-shouldered man with greying hair pushed

through the crowd and looked around. "You heard him, Kippy. Give."

The shill growled, tucked his knife away, reluctantly peeled a bill from a fat roll and handed it over.

The newcomer looked from Retief to Magnan.

"Pick another game, strangers," he said. "Kippy made a little mistake."

"This is small-time stuff," Retief said. "I'm interested in something big."

The broad-shouldered man lit a perfumed dope stick, then sniffed at it.

"What would you call big?" he said softly.

"What's the biggest you've got?"

The man narrowed his eyes, smiling. "Maybe you'd like to try Slam."

"Tell me about it."

"Over here." The crowd opened up and made a path. Retief and Magnan followed across the room to a brightly-lit glass-walled box. There was an arm-sized opening at waist height, and inside was a hand grip. A four-foot clear plastic globe a quarter full of chips hung in the center. Apparatus was mounted at the top of the box.

"Slam pays good odds," the man said. "You can go as high as you like. Chips cost you a hundred credits. You start it up by dropping a chip in here." He indicated a slot.

"You take the hand grip. When you squeeze, it unlocks and starts to turn. Takes a pretty good grip to start the globe turning. You can see, it's full of chips. There's a hole at the top. As long as you hold the grip, the bowl turns. The harder you squeeze, the faster it turns. Eventually it'll turn over to where the hole is down, and chips fall out. If you let up and the bowl stops, you're all through.

"Just to make it interesting, there's contact plates spotted around the bowl; when one of 'em lines up with a live contact, you get a little jolt—guaranteed non-lethal. But if you let go, you lose. All you've got to do is hold on long enough, and you'll get the pay-off."

"How often does this random pattern put the hole down?"

"Anywhere from three minutes to fifteen, with the average grip. Oh, by the way, one more thing. That lead block up there . . ." The man motioned with his head toward a one-foot cube suspended by a thick cable. "It's rigged to drop every now and then: averages five minutes. A warning light flashes first. You can set the clock back on it by dropping another chip—or you can let go the grip. Or you can take a chance; sometime's the light's a bluff."

Retief looked at the massive block of metal.

"That would mess up a man's dealing hand, wouldn't it?"

"The last two jokers who were too cheap to feed the machine had to have 'em off; their arm, I mean. That lead's heavy stuff."

"I don't suppose your machine has a habit of getting stuck, like Kippy's?"

The broad-shouldered man frowned.

"You're a stranger," he said. "You don't know any better."

"It's a fair game, mister," someone called.

"Where do I buy the chips?"

The man smiled. "I'll fix you up. How many?"

"One."

"A big spender, eh?" The man snickered and handed over a large plastic chip.

Retief stepped to the machine and dropped the coin.

"If you want to change your mind," the man said, "you can back out now. All it'll cost you is the chip you dropped."

Retief, reaching through the hole, took the grip. It was leather-padded, hand-filling. He squeezed it. There was a click and bright lights sprang up. The globe began to twirl lazily. The four-inch hole at its top was plainly visible.

"If ever the hole gets in position, it will empty very quickly," Magnan said.

Suddenly, a brilliant white light flooded the glass cage. A sound went up from the spectators.

"Quick, drop a chip," someone yelled.

"You've only got ten seconds . . ."

"Let go!" Magnan pleaded.

Retief sat silent, holding the grip, frowning up at the weight. The globe twirled faster now. Then the bright white light winked off.

"A bluff!" Magnan gasped.

"That's risky, stranger," the grey-templed man said.

The globe was turning rapidly now, oscillating from side to side. The hole seemed to travel in a wavering loop, dipping lower, swinging up high, then down again.

"It has to move to the bottom soon," Magnan said. "Slow it down, so it doesn't shoot past."

"The slower it goes, the longer it takes to get to the bottom," someone said.

There was a cackle, and Retief stiffened. Magnan

heard a sharp intake of breath. The globe slowed, and Retief shook his head, blinking.

The broad-shouldered man glanced at a meter.

"You took pretty near a full jolt, that time," he said.

The hole in the globe was tracing an oblique course now, swinging to the center, then below.

"A little longer," Magnan said.

"That's the best speed I ever seen on the Slam ball," someone said. "How much longer can he hold it?"

Magnan looked at Retief's knuckles. They showed white against the grip. The globe tilted farther, swung around, then down; two chips fell out, clattered down a chute and into a box.

"We're ahead," Magnan said. "Let's quit."

Retief shook his head. The globe rotated, dipped again; three chips fell.

"She's ready," someone called.

"It's bound to hit soon," another voice added excitedly. "Come on, mister!"

"Slow down," Magnan said. "So it won't move past too quickly."

"Speed it up. Before that lead block gets you," someone called.

The hole swung high, over the top, then down the side. Chips rained out, six, eight . . .

"Next pass," a voice called.

The white warning light flooded the cage. The globe whirled; the hole slid over the top, down down . . . a chip fell, two more . . .

Retief half rose, clamped his jaw, and crushed the grip. Sparks flew, and the globe slowed, chips spewing. It stopped and swung back. Weighted by the mass of chips at the bottom, it stopped again

with the hole centered. Chips cascaded down the
chute, filled the box and spilled on the floor. The
crowd yelled.

Retief released the grip and withdrew his arm at
the same instant that the lead block slammed down.

"Good lord," Magnan said. "I felt that through
the floor."

Retief turned to the broad-shouldered man.

"This game's all right for beginners," he said.
"But I'd like to talk a really big gamble. Why don't
we go to your office, Mr. Zorn?"

"Your proposition interests me," Zorn said, an
hour later. "But there's some angles to this I haven't
mentioned yet."

"You're a gambler, Zorn, not a suicide," Retief
said. "Take what I've offered. Your dream of revolution was fancier, I agree, but it won't work."

"How do I know you birds aren't lying?" Zorn
snarled. He stood up and strode up and down the
room. "You walk in here and tell me I'll have a
squadron of Corps Peace Enforcers on my neck,
that the Corps won't recognize my regime. Maybe
you're right; but I've got other contacts. They say
different." Whirling, he stared at Retief.

"I have pretty good assurance that once I put it
over, the Corps will have to recognize me as the
legal *de facto* government of Petreac. They won't
meddle in internal affairs."

"Nonsense," Magnan spoke up, "the Corps will
never deal with a pack of criminals calling themselves—"

"Watch your language, you!" Zorn rasped.

"I'll admit Mr. Magnan's point is a little weak,"
Retief said. "But you're overlooking something.

You plan to murder a dozen or so officers of the Corps Diplomatique Terrestrienne along with the local wheels. The Corps won't overlook that. It can't."

"Their tough luck they're in the middle," Zorn muttered.

"Our offer is extremely generous, Mr. Zorn," Magnan said. "The post you'll get will pay you very well indeed; as against certain failure of your coup, the choice should be simple."

Zorn eyed Magnan. "I thought you diplomats weren't the type to go around making deals under the table. Offering me a job—it sounds phony as hell."

"It's time you knew," Retief said. "There's no phonier business in the galaxy than diplomacy."

"You'd better take it, Mr. Zorn," Magnan said.

"Don't push me," Zorn said. "You two walk into my headquarters empty-handed and big-mouthed. I don't know what I'm talking to you for. The answer is no. N-i-x, no!"

"Who are you afraid of?" Retief said softly.

Zorn glared at him.

"Where do you get that 'afraid' routine? I'm top man here. What have I got to be afraid of?"

"Don't kid around, Zorn. Somebody's got you under his thumb. I can see you squirming from here."

"What if I let your boys alone?" Zorn said suddenly. "The Corps won't have anything to say then, huh?"

"The Corps has plans for Petreac, Zorn. You aren't part of them. A revolution right now isn't part of them. Having the Potentate and the whole

Nenni caste slaughtered isn't part of them. Do I make myself clear?"

"Listen," Zorn said urgently, "I'll tell you guys a few things. You ever heard of a world they call Rotune?"

"Certainly," Magnan said. "It's a near neighbor of yours, another backward—that is, emergent."

"Okay," Zorn said. "You guys think I'm a piker, do you? Well, let me wise you up. The Federal Junta on Rotune is backing my play. I'll be recognized by Rotune, and the Rotune fleet will stand by in case I need any help. I'll present the CDT with what you call a *fait accompli*."

"What does Rotune get out of this? I thought they were your traditional enemies."

"Don't get me wrong. I've got no use for Rotune; but our interests happen to coincide right now."

"Do they?" Retief smiled grimly. "You can spot a sucker as soon as he comes through that door out there—but you go for a deal like this."

"What do you mean?" Zorn looked angrily at Retief. "It's fool-proof."

"After you get in power, you'll be fast friends with Rotune, is that it?"

"Friends, hell. Just give me time to get set, and I'll square a few things with that—"

"Exactly. And what do you suppose they have in mind for you?"

"What are you getting at?"

"Why is Rotune interested in your take-over?"

Zorn studied Retief's face. "I'll tell you why," he said. "It's you birds; you and your trade agreement. You're here to tie Petreac into some kind of trade combine. That cuts Rotune out. They don't like that. And anyway, we're doing all right out here; we don't need any commitments to a lot of fancy-pants on the other side of the galaxy."

"That's what Rotune has sold you, eh?" Retief said, smiling.

"Sold, nothing—" Zorn ground out his dope stick, then lit another. He snorted angrily.

"Okay—what's your idea?"

"You know what Petreac is getting in the way of imports as a result of the trade agreement?"

"Sure, a lot of junk. Clothes washers, tape projectors, all that kind of stuff."

"To be specific," Retief said, "there'll be 50,000 Tatone B-3 dry washers; 100,000 Glo-float motile lamps; 100,000 Earthworm Minor garden cultivators; 25,000 Veco space heaters; and 75,000 replacement elements for Ford Monomeg drives."

"Like I said: a lot of junk," Zorn said.

Retief leaned back, looking sardonically at Zorn. "Here's the gimmick, Zorn," he said. "The Corps is getting a little tired of Petreac and Rotune carrying on their two-penny war out here. Your privateers have a nasty habit of picking on innocent bystanders. After studying both sides, the Corps has decided Petreac would be a little easier to do business with; so this trade agreement was worked out. The Corps can't openly sponsor an arms shipment to a belligerent; but personal appliances are another story."

"So what do we do—plow 'em under with backyard cultivators?" Zorn looked at Retief, puzzled. "What's the point?"

"You take the sealed monitor unit from the washer, the repeller field generator from the lamp, the converter control from the cultivator, et cetera, et cetera. You fit these together according to some very simple instructions; presto! you have one hundred thousand Standard-class Y hand blasters; just the thing to turn the tide in a stalemated war fought with obsolete arms."

"Good Lord," Magnan said. "Retief, are you—"

"I have to tell him. He has to know what he's putting his neck into."

"Weapons, hey?" Zorn said. "And Rotune knows about it. . . ?"

"Sure they know about it; it's not too hard to figure out. And there's more. They want the CDT delegation included in the massacre for a reason; it will put Petreac out of the picture; the trade agreement will go to Rotune; and you and your new regime will find yourselves looking down the muzzles of your own blasters."

Zorn threw his dope-stick to the floor with a snarl.

"I should have smelled something when that Rotune agent made his pitch." Zorn looked at the clock on the wall.

"I've got two hundred armed men in the palace. We've got about forty minutes to get over there before the rocket goes up."

In the shadows of the palace terrace, Zorn turned to Retief. "You'd better stay here out of the way until I've spread the word. Just in case."

"Let me caution you against any . . . ah . . . slip-ups, Mr. Zorn," Magnan said. "The Nenni are not to be molested."

Zorn looked at Retief. "Your friend talks too much. I'll keep my end of it; he'd better keep his."

"Nothing's happened yet, you're sure?" Magnan said.

"I'm sure," Zorn said. "Ten minutes to go; plenty of time."

"I'll just step into the salon to assure myself that all is well," Magnan said.

"Suit yourself. Just stay clear of the kitchen, or you'll get your throat cut." Zorn smiled at his dope-stick. "I sent the word for Shoke," he muttered. "Wonder what's keeping him?"

Magnan stepped to a tall glass door, eased it open, and poked his head through the heavy draperies. As he moved to draw back, a voice was faintly audible. Magnan paused, his head still through the drapes.

"What's going on there?" Zorn rasped. He and Retief stepped up behind Magnan.

". . . breath of air," Magnan was saying.

"Well, come along, Magnan!" Ambassador Crodfoller's voice snapped.

Magnan shifted from one foot to the other, then pushed through the drapes.

"Where've you been, Mr. Magnan?" The ambassador's voice was sharp.

"Oh . . . ah . . . a slight accident, Mr. Ambassador."

"What's happened to your shoes? Where are your insignia and decorations?"

"I—ah—spilled a drink on them. Maybe I'd better nip up to my room and slip into some fresh medals."

The ambassador snorted. "A professional diplomat never shows his liquor, Magnan. It's one of his primary professional skills. I'll speak to you about this later. I had expected your attendance at the signing ceremony, but under the circumstances I'll dispense with that. You'd better depart quietly through the kitchen."

"The kitchen? But it's crowded . . . I mean . . ."

"A little loss of caste won't hurt at this point, Mr. Magnan. Now kindly move along before you attract attention. The agreement isn't signed yet."

"The agreement . . ." Magnan babbled, sparring for time, "very clear, Mr. Ambassador. A very neat solution."

The sound of an orchestra came up suddenly, blaring a fanfare.

Zorn shifted restlessly, his ear against the glass. "What's your friend pulling?" he rasped. "I don't like this."

"Keep cool, Zorn. Mr. Magnan is doing a little emergency salvage on his career."

The music died away with a clatter.

". . . my God." Ambassador Crodfoller's voice was faint. "Magnan, you'll be knighted for this. Thank God you reached me. Thank God it's not too late. I'll find some excuse. I'll get off a gram at once."

"But you—"

"It's all right, Magnan. You were in time. Another ten minutes and the agreement would have been signed and transmitted. The wheels would have been put in motion. My career would have been ruined. . . ."

Retief felt a prod at his back. He turned.

"Double-crossed," Zorn said softly. "So much for the word of a diplomat."

Retief looked at the short-barreled needler in Zorn's hand.

"I see you hedge your bets, Zorn."

"We'll wait here until the excitement's over inside. I wouldn't want to attract any attention right now."

"Your politics are still lousy, Zorn. The picture hasn't changed. Your coup hasn't got a chance."

"Skip it. I'll take up one problem at a time."

"Magnan's mouth has a habit of falling open at the wrong time."

"That's my good luck I heard it. So there'll be no agreement, no guns, no fat job for Tammany Zorn, hey? Well, I can still play it the other way. What have I got to lose?"

With a movement too quick to follow, Retief's hand chopped down across Zorn's wrist. The needler clattered to the ground as Retief's hand clamped on Zorn's arm, whirling him around.

"In answer to your last question," Retief said, "your neck."

"You haven't got a chance, double-crosser," Zorn gasped.

"Shoke will be here in a minute. Tell him it's all off."

"Twist harder, mister. Break it off at the shoulder. I'm telling him nothing."

"The kidding's over, Zorn. Call it off or I'll kill you."

"I believe you. But you won't have long to remember it."

"All the killing will be for nothing. You'll be dead and the Rotunes will step into the power vacuum."

"So what? When I die, the world ends."

"Suppose I make you another offer, Zorn?"

"Why would it be any better than the last one?"

Retief released Zorn's arm, pushed him away, stooped and picked up the needler.

"I could kill you, Zorn; you know that."

"Go ahead."

Retief reversed the needler and held it out.

"I'm a gambler too, Zorn. I'm gambling you'll listen to what I have to say."

Zorn snatched the gun and stepped back. He looked at Retief. "That wasn't the smartest bet you ever made, but go ahead. You've got maybe ten seconds."

"Nobody double-crossed you, Zorn. Magnan put his foot in it; too bad. Is that a reason to kill yourself and a lot of other people who've bet their lives on you?"

"They gambled and lost. Tough."

"Maybe they haven't lost yet—if you don't quit."

"Get to the point."

Retief spoke earnestly for a minute and a half. Zorn stood, gun aimed, listening. Then both men turned as footsteps approached along the terrace. A fat man in a yellow sarong padded up to Zorn.

Zorn tucked the needler in his waistband.

"Hold everything, Shoke," he said. "Tell the boys to put the knives away; spread the word fast: it's all off."

"I want to commend you, Retief," Ambassador Crodfoller said expansively. "You mixed very well at last night's affair; actually, I was hardly aware of your presence."

"I've been studying Mr. Magnan's work," Retief said.

"A good man, Magnan. In a crowd, he's virtually invisible."

"He knows when to disappear, all right."

"This has been in many ways a model operation, Retief." The ambassador patted his paunch contentedly. "By observing local social customs and blending harmoniously with the court, I've succeeded in establishing a fine, friendly, working relationship with the Potentate."

"I understand the agreement has been postponed a few days."

The Ambassador chuckled. "The Potentate's a crafty one. Through . . . ah . . . a special study I have been conducting, I learned last night that he had hoped to, shall I say, 'put one over' on the Corps."

"Great Heavens," Retief said.

"Naturally, this placed me in a difficult position. It was my task to quash this gambit, without giving any indication that I was aware of its existence."

"A hairy position indeed."

"Quite casually, I informed the Potentate that certain items which had been included in the terms of the agreement had been deleted and others substituted. I admired him at that moment, Retief. He took it coolly—appearing completely indifferent—perfectly dissembling his very serious disappointment. Of course, he could hardly do otherwise without in effect admitting his plot."

"I noticed him dancing with three girls each wearing a bunch of grapes; he's very agile for a man of his bulk."

"You mustn't discount the Potentate. Remember, beneath that mask of frivolity, he had absorbed a bitter blow."

"He had me fooled," Retief said.

"Don't feel badly; I confess at first I, too, failed

to sense his shrewdness." The ambassador nodded
and moved off along the corridor.

Retief turned and went into an office. Magnan
looked up from his desk.

"Ah, Retief," he said. "I've been meaning to ask
you. About the . . . ah, blasters; are you—"

Retief leaned on Magnan's desk and looked at
him. "I thought that was to be our little secret."

"Well, naturally I—" Magnan closed his mouth
and swallowed. "How is it, Retief," he said sharply,
"that you were aware of this blaster business, when
the ambassador himself wasn't?"

"Easy," Retief said. "I made it up."

"You what!" Magnan looked wild. "But the
agreement—it's been revised. Ambassador Crodfoller has gone on record."

"Too bad. Glad I didn't tell him about it."

Magnan leaned back and closed his eyes.

"It was big of you to take all the . . . blame,"
Retief said, "when the ambassador was talking about
knighting people."

Magnan opened his eyes. "What about that gambler, Zorn? Won't he be upset when he learns the
agreement is off? After all, I . . . that is, we, or
you, had more or less promised him—"

"It's all right. I made another arrangement. The
business about making blasters out of common
components wasn't completely imaginary. You can
actually do it, using parts from an old-fashioned
disposal unit."

"What good will that do him?" Magnan whispered, looking nervous. "We're not shipping in
any old-fashioned disposal units."

"We don't need to. They're already installed in

the palace kitchen—and in a few thousand other places, Zorn tells me."

"If this ever leaks . . ." Magnan put a hand to his forehead.

"I have his word on it that the Nenni slaughter is out. This place is ripe for a change; maybe Zorn is what it needs."

"But how can we know?" Magnan said. "How can we be sure?"

"We can't. But it's not up to the Corps to meddle in Petreac's internal affairs." He leaned over, picked up Magnan's desk lighter, and lit a cigar. He blew a cloud of smoke toward the ceiling.

"Right?" he said.

Magnan looked at him and nodded weakly. "Right."

"I'd better be getting along to my desk," Retief said. "Now that the ambassador feels that I'm settling down at last."

"Retief," Magnan said, "tonight, I implore you: stay out of the kitchen—no matter what."

Retief raised his eyebrows.

"I know," Magnan said. "If you hadn't interfered, we'd all have had our throats cut. But at least . . ." He paused, "we'd have died in accordance with regulations."

Rank Injustice

1

The ten-thousand-tonner *Expedient*, on lease to the Interplanetary Tribunal for Curtailment of Hostilities, was holed by a six-ton slab of nickle-iron just as the four hundred assorted diplomatic staff members aboard, from as many worlds, were taking cocktails in the main lounge, in expectation of planetfall within the hour. The shock, far aft, rattled ice-cubes and sent trays of glasses sliding along the hundred-foot heowood bar, dumping a beaker of Lovenbroy pale ale into the lap of First Secretary and Consul Ben Magnan, who leaped up with a shrill cry.

"Retief! That confounded chief engineer is inebriated again! I distinctly felt the jar as he mistimed his power change-over to atmospheric!"

"Maybe," Retief conceded. "But I'm afraid it's something more serious this time."

"What could be more serious than a drunken powerman in charge of re-entry?"

"A collision," Retief told him. "A mere bobble in thrust timing wouldn't open a seam in the bulkhead." Magnan followed his glance toward a rent in the brocade wallpaper.

"A collision!" Magnan yelled before Retief could stop him. At once the cry was taken up by those near-by, who finished their drinks at a gulp and rushed off in all directions to spread the word.

"Where's the captain?" demanded a gaunt mantis-like female counsellor from Glory Eleven in a voice that cut across the rising tumult like a meat-saw.

"I *demand* to know what he's doing about this catastrophe!" she added, in case anyone was in doubt. She stood with two pairs of arms folded, staring around defiantly, until her gaze fell on Retief and Magnan. "You!" she yelped. "You people are Terrans like captain! What are doing to save innocent lives?"

"While, Madam," Magnan began, "I cheerfully acknowledge the accuracy of your charge that my assistant and I indeed share with Captain Suggs the honor of being Terrans, we are in no way involved in the operation of this vessel. Anyway," he added less graciously, "I don't see any innocent lives being threatened."

"You dismiss all these selfless diplomats as guilty?" the lady demanded, even more shrilly. "And of *what*, may I inquire?"

"You mistake my meaning, Madam," Magnan gobbled. "I have leveled no accusation against those present! Like yourself, I cry our captain culpable! Wherever *is* the scamp?"

"This here Terry done called Captain Suggs a scamp," someone commented loudly.

Retief touched Magnan's arm. "Let's go, Mr. Magnan," he suggested. "You're in a classic no-win situation."

"Go where?" Magnan demanded, bewildered. "We're trapped here aboard this frail perfidious bark just like everyone else! Unless, of course, you were thinking of taking to the lifeboats . . . ?"

"Back to take a look at the damage," Retief explained. "That was an impact aft, I think."

"In that case one would be mad to go aft!" Magnan objected. "If we're holed, there'll be no atmosphere!"

"We'll freeze before we asphyxiate," Retief pointed out. "Unless we aren't really holed—or if we suit up."

The irate Glorytian lady had stamped off in a huff and was eagerly collaring other bewildered passengers to demand action.

"There he is, the incompetent!" she interrupted herself to yell, as Captain Suggs hove into view from the crowd, a slight, rather bedraggled figure in soiled whites with four tarnished gold stripes, his face unshaven.

"Whassamare?" he demanded cheerfully, skillfully scooping a full glass from an adjacent table, at the same time depositing an empty. A moment later, he discarded another empty. "I gotta order all you good folks to disperse," he called to no one in particular. "Now, you, over there . . ." he waved in Magnan's general direction as the latter approached him. "Mister Magnan, ain't it? Used to be good on names, Mr. Mumble. You're a Terry like me. I hereby appoint you to head up a panel to investigate whatever clobbered my command here. Aft. We been struck aft," he elaborated.

"Pretty good smack, too, registered prolly a few tons doing twenty thou or better." He turned abruptly and bolted, shooing confused bureaucrats from his path, ignoring the chorus of complaints.

"Why, the man is drunk, like his Powerman," Magnan commented in an awed tone, as he returned to Retief's side. "I shouldn't wonder if he isn't personally responsible for the malfunction, whatever it is."

"He's had a few," Retief agreed, "but he's spent forty years in space; when he says a few tons of something have hit us, I'm inclined to believe him."

"Oh, dear," Magnan moaned, then, more decisively, "But that's highly unlikely. I read somewhere that the density of matter in interplanetary space in this system is about like six jelly-flies in Marsport's Grand Concourse! Still, it's Captain Suggs's responsibility, and he's doing nothing!"

"I guess that's something, ain't it, Mr. Magnan?" Suggs's blurry voice spoke up from just behind Magnan. "When doing nothing is the best thing to do, I do it!"

"You call doing nothing doing something?" Magnan demanded, whirling to confront the Skipper.

"Sure," Suggs acknowledged cheerfully. "Can't take her into atmosphere if she ain't spaceworthy, and our best bet is just to stay in parking orbit until they send a damage-control party up to fix everything. Already got off a distress bleep," he added. "Asked for approach number, too; they tole me to stay put."

"Stay put?" Magnan echoed. "Do you realize, sir, that in mere minutes an ITCH conference of stupendous importance is about to begin without me?"

"Guess keeping alive until he'p gets here is more important than your eczema," Suggs commented indifferently. "So long, Mr. Magnan, see you around—and go see my pharmacist's mate; he'll fix that rash."

" 'Rash,' indeed!" Magnan burst out. He turned to Retief. "Retief!" he hissed. "I'm surprised that in this moment of crisis you're as passive as the rest! I expected that at the least you'd nip aft and look into the captain's allegation that we've been involved in a collision!"

"Aren't you coming along, sir?" Retief asked as he put his glass on a passing tray. Magnan recoiled as if from a blast of wintry air.

"Hardly!" he huffed. "My place as Transit Director is here, maintaining order until you return to report that all is well. Listen to them," he switched subjects with breathtaking agility. "They're already at daggers drawn over who's to take charge! Pushy of them, when it's clear you have them all outranked, if not in your diplomatic status as a lowly Foreign Service Officer of Class Two, then in your position as Chief of the Armed Forces of your native world!"

Several sets of eyes, some stalked, others recessed light-sensitive pores, turned toward the two Terrans.

A large man with crooked teeth stepped forward; Magnan turned away after a single disapproving glance.

"Kouth is the handle," the newcomer said in a gravelly bass voice which seemed to reverberate

among the chandeliers. "You can call me 'Boss.'"
Magnan drew back hastily.

"'Kouth' may be, as he says, the name," he
commented to no one in particular, "but *not* the
manner."

"Skip that, Bub," Kouth rumbled. "What we got
to do, we got to set this here tub down on the
inner moon. That's why I'm taking over." His gaze
shifted to Retief. "You look like a pretty strong
boy," he commented. "So you'll be my First Mate.
Now, we better amble on back up to the bridge
and set course fer Old Moon."

"Here, fellow!" piped a small, cootie-like chap
in elaborate diplomatic formal dress, as he popped
up between the two much larger beings.

"I'm Ambassador Phoop," he clarified. "And as
senior Career Ambassador aboard, I outrank all of
these military chaps; why, even a mere Career
Minister ranks with and after a buck general." In a
less heated tone, he continued: "First, I must
organize you, and dispatch a damage-control party.
You—" he pointed at Kouth's knee, "—and you as
well," he added as he stepped back to stare up at
Retief's six-foot-three towering over him. "You two
lads are hereby designated as top sergeants to
shape up this mob into squads of ten individuals,
regardless of species, pigmentation, or mystical
alignment with regard to the Big Goober in the
Sky."

"To fail to grasp the enormity of your cheek,
Mr. Ambassador," a breathy Groaci voice spoke in
the local stunned near-silence which had followed
Phoop's pronouncement. "To admire the breath-
taking audacity of such a claim to primacy," the
Groaci went on, "but of course I as an Assistant

UnderSecretary to Foreign Affairs, am senior diplomat aboard this vessel and as such naturally take command during the indisposition of Captain Suggs!"

"Unspeakable!" Ambassador Phoop squeaked. "It was none other than yourself, Mr. Secretary, who plied our captain with strong drink, which I myself abjure, of course, thus rendering him incapacitated in this hour of crisis!"

"What do your curious drinking habits have to do with Captain Suggs's lack of competence, small sir?" A grossly rotund Vorplisher demanded, then turned his attention to sampling the foam on a tankard of ale. "I'm Major General Blow," he added, "and I'm in command here."

"You distort my meaning, sir!" Phoop squeaked, ignoring the general. "*I* had nothing to do with this Suggs's dereliction of duty!"

"This here is all academic like they say," Kouth put in bluntly. "This here is *my* turf; I'm a Stugger borned and bred, whatever that is, which that's the planet Stug figuratively like looming up on the hypothetical forward screens at the moment. I and my boys are the only native-borned Stuggies aboard, so I'm in charge here. Any objections, any of youse pansies?"

"Plenty!" Major General Blow boomed as he charged, impacting Kouth like a runaway fork-lift colliding with a semi loaded with gravel. Kouth responded by backing into a table covered with trays of empties, then hoisted the belligerent Vorplisher above his head and threw him into the faces of the fascinated onlookers.

"Some guys has wrong ideas about when to get

tough," he commented. "Now the rest o' you recruits line up agin the wall over there!"

" 'Wall,' indeed!" an ornately-uniformed spider-lean fellow from Wolf Nine, a minor world listed as Booch in the New Catalog, spoke up indignantly. "It's clear, sir, you are unqualified to serve as a deck-swabber last class, to say nothing of assuming command of a deep-space vessel in dire distress! In navel parlance that's called a 'bulkhead'," he finished quite calmly.

After a moment of silence, punctuated by a single "'ear, 'ear!" from somewhere back in the crowd, the skinny chap went on:

"I myself am Grand Captain of Avenging Flotillas Blance, representing the Boochian Combined Armed Forces. It is clear that no one here can challenge my credentials as ranking Being aboard!" He stepped out of line, leaned tête-à-tête with another of like physique, then made shooing motions.

"What I hear," a squat, burly, green-furred code clerk attached to the Hondu Military Attache put in, "Booch ain't *got* no navy. Nor no other armed forces, neither."

"What is at issue here, my man—" Phoop started, only to be cut off by the Hondu with a peremptory gesture.

"I ain't no man, Cap, and I shore ain't yourn!" he corrected the diplomat.

"—is not a comparative assessment of military appropriations," Phoop continued, undaunted, "but a simple matter of personal rank."

"A Grand Captain of an imaginary fleet don't outrank a Deck-swabber Last Class in a first-class fighting outfit," the Hondu declared, "Like me. So you can go into a early retirement, Admiral, DS-LC Gloon is here!"

Before Grand Captain Blance could reply, he was thrust aside unceremoniously by Kouth, who in turn was jostled by General Blow as both contenders for leadership stepped forward to advance their claims.

"We set her down nice and easy on Old Moon," Kouth declared loudly.

"I have determined—" General Blow began, only to be cut off by Admiral Blance.

"A land-lubber, though of two-star rank, has no place in command in space!" he stated, but his further remarks were cut short when Gloon elbowed the wafer-thin Boochian, then to his astonishment was at once knocked flat by a snake-swift blow from the Grand Captain.

"You will not venture again to lay hands on the person of a Boochian Grand Captain," the indignant officer said harshly.

"I never laid no hand on nobody," Gloon objected as he regained his feet with an assist from a slightly smaller Hondu in NCO whites. "All I laid on you was a elbow!"

"The principle is the same, DS-LC!" Blance dismissed the matter. "Now, I think you may as well take charge of that half of this mob of civilians, and form up in a column of ducks!"

"I don't guess no DS-LC is gonna fall me in," General Blow objected. "I done my basic thirty years ago, and I demand—"

What the general would have demanded was not to be known, as at that moment the hitherto relatively orderly crowd dissolved into a melee, as officious drill sergeants spot-promoted by half a dozen competing captains *pro tem* attempted to form the rank-conscious civilian diplomats into manageable units, Kouth's polyglot supporter being the most vocal.

Magnan clutched at Retief's sleeve. "Now, for sure, it's time to slip away," he summarized. "And I've decided, yes, I shall accompany you. I don't care for that Kouth person at all. So, shall we?"

2

"It's as good a time as any," Retief agreed, fending off a belligerent Yillian with ornate rank badges, sending him reeling into a fist-fight, in which the grey-skinned flag officer cheerfully joined.

"This is all most unseemly!" Magnan exclaimed, stepping aside barely in time to avoid being swept up in a three-being wrestling match. "As designated Director of this party, I myself—"

"Forget it, Ben," a lowly Terran corporal of the Jawbone Planetary Defense Force advised just before he was struck down by a Haterakan supreme Overlord of Irresistible Armadas, a rank equivalent to a Bloovian maker of ritual Grimaces, Third Class, Magnan noted.

"Cheeky to a degree," Magnan sniffed, slapping the hypothetical dust of the near-encounter from the lapels of his Late Early Mid-morning cutaway. "It's no wonder," he added in an aside to Retief, "that Sector has reported piracy and wreckers operating in this region, if that Boss Kouth is any example of the local ruling class."

"I heard that crack, Ben," a nosy Groaci Consular Officer informed the Terran. "If you Ter-

ries are so worried about dacoits and corsairs operating in Stuggish space, hows come you decided to
stage this ITCH convention right here in the middle of No Being's Land, hah?"

"Simplicity itself, Thiss," Magnan replied loft-
ily. "It is precisely because this region is a hotbed
of deep-space crime that we selected it as the
appropriate site for talks designed to diminish that
very problem."

"Hold! Enough!" a deep voice boomed out. All
eyes turned toward a two-ton Fustian elder who
had risen from his usual torpor to loom over the
lesser beings all around him.

"I," he stated, "am Field Marshall Whelk, and if
it's rank you're looking for, I've got rank I haven't
even used yet. Get thee hence, all but you—" he
pointed a stubby but massive clawed hand at
Kouth—"and you—and you," designated the Hondu
spac'n as well as Admiral Phoop. "You fellows are
my lieutenants," he explained in a tone which
invited no discussion. "Now restore order here,
and do it quietly."

"I tell ya we gotta make fer Old Moon," Kouth
stated boldly. He turned to address his appeal to
the raggedly formed-up crowd, Whelk having already resumed his slumber. "It's our only chancet!" Kouth declared.

"And I say we hold orbit like the cap'n said!"
someone rebutted from the rear rank. "Rescue
party's on the way!" A barrel-shaped, deep-blue
Krakan swaggered forth to confront Kouth.

Kouth motioned, and half a dozen of his adherents emerged from the crowd to surround the
Krakan. While everyone was engrossed in the power
struggle, Magnan ducked out a side door and Retief
accompanied him.

3

The passage leading aft past Stores to Power Section was silent and deserted. Then a big spac'n in soiled whites with the nine blue stripes of a Chief Master Spaceman First, Stuggish Merchant Marine, stepped from a side passage and came toward the two civilians.

"No crust-huggers allowed here," he announced in a tone of weary authority, then halted, blocking the passage. "I'm McCluskey," he added. "*Chief* McCluskey, to you."

"Where did it hit?" Magnan inquired in a tone which was almost a squeak. "Do step aside, my man," he went on, "we're on our way to inspect the damage."

"I guess maybe you don't hear so good, chum," the Chief announced. "I tole youse onct, no civilians in my Power Section, OK? So you better just turn around and tip-toe back to yer easy chairs. Now, before I start to get annoyed and all."

"Do step aside, I say, fellow," Magnan repeated. "We've no time for gossip just now."

"Oh, yeah?" the powerman came back truculently. "Well, I'm telling you, Junior, you got no business here aft. Youse could get hurt. Hot stuff could be sloshing around all over the place. Shoo! Leave us pros deal with this here."

" 'Might be,' you say," Magnan echoed. "I think we need a trifle more specific assessment of the status than that." Magnan paused, then clutched Retief's arm. "Goodness," he gushed. "What if this gorilla is right? We could receive a fatal blast of radiation as soon as we open the hard-seal doors."

McCluskey advanced a step toward Magnan, seeming, as he did so, to expand to fill the narrow passage. "I guess you never called me a gorilla," he commented mildly.

" 'Guerilla,' " Magnan corrected breathlessly. "An heroic freedom fighter, that is. One mustn't go putting words in the mouths of others," he added.

McCluskey showed Magnan a fist as big as a cabbage. "It ain't words I'm thinking of putting in yer mush, Cull, and I never fought no freedom. You got two seconds; one t'ousan and one, a t'ousan an two—"

Magnan turned to flee, but rebounded from Retief and staggered back directly into the big powerman, who fended him off, looking puzzled.

"Never figgered the little shrimp to charge me," he mused aloud. "Backwards, too. Must be some new kinda martial arts for weaklings or like that." He picked Magnan up and paused as if uncertain what to do next.

"You'd better put Mr. Magnan down, Chief," Retief suggested gently. "Otherwise he might decide to unleash his ire on you."

"Where?" McCluskey looked over, through, and past Retief. "I don't see no leashed ire, nor no other kind neither. Had a pal once, had this here catamount on a leash, spose to be trained and all. Onney one day it got hungry and ate my pal's leg off before he could remember to say 'heel.' "

"That's a very melancholy anecdote, Chief," Retief said. "Now, about the damage aft. What hit us? And precisely where? Did it penetrate the impact hull? Is there any radioactive leakage?"

"Well, now, just a minute, Bud. What hit us, we got clobbered by a iron-nickle, looks like, and it come through the hull, all three layers and the containment bulkhead and busted the coolant system wide open, after which I didn't see no more, cause I still plan to get hitched some day and father some little deckhands, which I don't want 'em to have two heads and all."

"Reasonable enough, Chief," Retief acknowledged. "But suppose we just suit up and go take a closer look."

"Well, old Cap Suggs will split a gusset when he hears about it," the Chief grumped. "But I guess somebody got to do somethin. So, OK. Equipment lockers is right over there."

Minutes later all three men were fully clad in what McCluskey referred to as 'lead underwear.' Magnan complained bitterly at the poor fit and excessive weight of the R-garment, a Mark XV.

"One can't even breathe in this contraption," he carped. "To say nothing of walking, not to mention doing anything useful."

"Why don't you just lie down here," Retief suggested, indicating a long, padded table intended for use during fitting of the custom-tailored suits. "The Chief and I will handle it."

"Hey, I just come to think," McCluskey interjected. "I ain't said youse are goin' *in* there with me. The both of youse better wait right here. I'll take a quick look-see and let you know what the status is."

Retief went past the Chief's bulky, R-suited figure, and cycled the entry hatch into Power Section. McCluskey, still objecting, followed. Magnan lay back with a groan.

"Hurry, Retief," he called after his departing colleague. "I'm sure I'm going to suffocate if I'm not released from this strait-jacket within the minute."

Retief paused to call over his shoulder. "Just take deep breaths, Mr. Magnan. I'll be back before you know it."

"Unless these gammas get to you, first," McCluskey added cheerfully as he clanged the hatch behind him.

Retief went across to the gaping frost-rimmed rent caused by the entry of the object the ship had struck; it was approximately sealed by a slab of tough, versatile plastron, which had been slapped in place by the automatics immediately after the penetration.

"That there rubber'll hold OK for a hour or two, maybe, before it cryodegrades," McCluskey estimated. "Before then what I got to do, I got to get a class three temporary in there."

"Meanwhile," Retief told him, "you'd better start up the contain-and-exhaust gear."

"Sure," the chief acknowledged. "I was goin' to."

"That why you were out in the passage, headed forward?" Retief inquired pointedly.

"That sounds to me like some kind of crack," McCluskey announced, and moved toward Retief with one large, gauntleted fist cocked. Retief pushed his clumsy swing aside and said, "Tsk, naughty. The C and E, remember?" The big spacer moved on, muttering. Retief studied the trajectory of the missile, clearly marked by a swath of cut pipes, conduits and cables, all leading to the missile itself, half-buried in the massive casting which housed the converter gear. He went over and looked at the slab of partly-melted iron, deep-pocked and porous, perforated by melt-holes and somewhat flattened on one side by the impact. It was warm to the touch. He turned to a wall-mounted cabinet, snapped the cover open and looked over the array of tools and equipment inside, then selected a sharp-tipped sampler and gouged a tiny fragment from the metal slab, leaving a bright scar. He put the sample in the mass spectrograph from the cabinet and waited for a read-out, jotted it down and called to McCluskey:

"Has anybody touched this thing?"

"Naw," the chief replied. "See, I was too busy to mess with it."

"Busy not cycling the spill out, eh?" Retief suggested.

"Get offa my back, for cripesakes," McCluskey came back. "Now I ain't kidding no more. You gotta get outta here, I don't mean later."

"As it happens, Chief," Retief replied casually, "I was just going forward."

"You can tell that so-called captain that Chief McCluskey has got matters well in hand aft," the belligerent powerman stated.

Abruptly, the squawk-box crackled and spoke: "Now hear this! This here is Field-Marshall—"

"Skip that," another voice cut in. "I'm Under-Secretary Frunch, and I'm ordering all hands to take to the lifeboats! Abandon ship!"

"As you were, passengers and crew," a glutinous voice countermanded the Secretary's order. "What we got to do, we got to put her down on Old Moon, like Mr. Kouth said, so—"

"Nonsense!" a faint Groaci voice dismissed the

suggestion. "To man battle stations, all crew; and all passengers to their staterooms, in an orderly fashion, mind you!"

"Why don't them bums get with the program?" McCluskey demanded of the circumambient air. "It's Old Moon, just like Boss Kouth said!" He broke off to stare as if astonished as Retief paused by the power control panel and began throwing switches. "Hey!" he yelled. "What you think you're doing?" He charged, but somehow collided helmet-first with the panel as Retief palmed him off gently and stepped aside. McCluskey slid to the deck, half-stunned; as he groped to get all fours under him, Retief grabbed his helmet by the cluster of cables emerging from its top and slammed the fellow's head against the panel again. McCluskey went limp. Retief went on with his resetting of the panel. After a few seconds, the fallen space'n raised his head:

"Yer setting up for re-entry," he objected. "No atmosphere on Old Moon, and besides that you got no call to mess around here in my power section!"

"One more time, Chief?" Retief inquired inter-estedly as he once again took a grip on McCluskey's helmet.

"Naw, I got no beef," the latter protested. "I already got a broke moobie-bone prolly. But tryna set this bucket down on a plus-G world with her hull broached is suicide. Have a heart, Bub, and leave it lay!"

Retief dropped the Chief's head with a dull *clang!* and left the compartment. Magnan was wait-ing impatiently, having removed his G-suit.

"I suppose it was nothing after all," he caroled. "Where's Chief McCluskey?"

"He's lying down," Retief told him.

"Oh, no doubt quite tuckered after his ordeal, poor fellow," Magnan guessed. "But he seems to have done his duty before resting. We must remember to mention his coolness in the emergency in our dispatches."

"Just one thing, Mr. Magnan," Retief cut in on his supervisor's dythrambics. "It was no accident. That supposed meteoric iron has a 1.738 percent carbon content, precisely that of standard industrial steel."

"No!" Magnan gasped. "Whyever would anyone want to fake a disaster in space?"

"The disaster's genuine," Retief told him. "It's just the meteoroid that's a fake. And judging by the angle of entry and the size of the hole, its relative velocity was zero point zero."

"You mean it was stationary?" Magnan yelped. "But that's impossible! It would have been falling toward Stug, at escape velocity at the very least!"

"Unless someone had just dropped it off squarely in our projected path," Retief corrected.

"We must notify Captain Suggs at once!" Magnan declared.

In the equipment bay, having returned his G-suit to its locker, Retief looked over the items stored in the adjacent cabinet, selected a late-model crater-gun, strapped it on, and dumped the rest of the arms in the recycler.

"Retief!" Magnan cried, "whatever *do* you intend? Bearing arms is hardly consonant with normal diplomatic procedure!"

"Neither is Kouth," Retief pointed out, "nor the

rest of these king-makers, either. But I'll put it up my sleeve if that will make you feel better."

"Must you jape, even in the cannon's mouth?" Magnan demanded in an outraged tone, as he hurried off along the passage.

As they reached the axial lift, it *bang!*ed open and a disheveled Zooner pre-adult floated out, drifting with the air currents a few inches clear of the floor.

"I suppose," it began in an irritable tone, "that you people are adherents of that uncouth Vreeb person. Well, you may as well know—I'm a partisan of Captain Hoshoon."

"Never heard of him, sir or madam," Magnan hastened to declare. "Have you seen the captain, by any chance?"

"Depends on who you mean by 'captain,' " the partly-shedding creature replied, pausing to scratch its blue-furred back against the lift frame and dislodging another patch of the hairy juvenile pelt. "Itch is driving me crazy," it vouchsafed. "Looks to me like Hoshoon has the power, since Admiral Phoop threw his weight behind him."

"We really must rush off," Magnan gabbled, "if you'd be so kind as to excuse us, madam or sir."

"Ain't neither the one nor the other, till after the moult," the unhappy Zooner grumped.

"One wonders," Magnan confided to Retief as the lift door closed off his view of the shedding alien, "just what animus the creature holds against the Tribunal."

"I think it was itch, not ITCH, it was carping about," Retief suggested. The speaker in the car's ceiling cleared its throat and intoned, sounding bored:

"Tole all personnel to assemble on the boat deck in half a squat," it said, in Boss Kouth's voice.

"It's Kouth!" Magnan exclaimed.

"Damn right!" the voice confirmed. "After I finished off that Krakan wiseguy, I done talked some sense into these slobs and now we can get busy and get this here wreck down on Old Moon before she breaks up. Bad business, a piece o' arn size of a sofa cushion in yer Power Section. Over and out and all that stuff."

"Heavens!" Magnan remarked. "Candidly, I doubt that Mr. Kouth is competent to command *Expedient*. And whyever do you suppose they've elected him captain?"

"Who said anything about electing?" Kouth demanded. "And I heard that crack about me being a incompetent and all. Well, I guess I'm competent enough to shape up this here bunch of dithering diplomats! And if ya wanna utter like sedition in secret, ya better switch off the talker."

"That is hardly the point, Captain Kouth," Magnan rebuked the volunteer skipper. "I trust you've at least retained Captain Suggs in an advisory capacity. After all, he knows the vessel."

"He's sleeping it off in the dispensary," Kouth dismissed the matter abruptly. "Now you better get yer butt back up here on the double; and tell McCluskey he's busted back to Log Room Yeoman fer letting youse in Power Section. Out and over!"

The lift having reached the end of the line, they debarked and started up the narrow companionway to Command Section. Halfway up, the Hondu Deck-swabber Last Class, Gloon, came tumbling down, slack, his green fur matted with ochre blood. Magnan ducked back as the bulky Hondu fell toward him. "Horrid!" he gasped. "And what an appalling color combination!

"Good lord, Retief," he moaned, shrinking back to give the shaggy body the widest possible berth as it fell past him, "I feared it would come to this. Fortunate indeed that I directed you to arm yourself—for self and supervisor—defense only, of course. Very well," he added, more calmly, "You may proceed now—but cautiously, mind you. There's a murderer up there."

Thumping sounds from above seemed to confirm Magnan's deduction. Retief drew his gun and waved Magnan back. He went up to the final dogged-shut hatch to the sacrosanct Control Deck. Beyond it, faint scuffling noises were audible, interspersed with muttered obscenities and an occasional louder thump such as Magnan had heard from below. Then the hatch clicked and cycled open a few inches. Captain Suggs's bleary visage peered down at Retief.

"Good thing you come along, feller," the skipper mumbled. "Had one o' them green spacers up here to help me; good hand, too, but he tried to get insubordinate on me, and I hadda coldcock him." He displayed a heavy spanner with a smear of ochre on its one-and-three-eighths end.

Retief climbed up inside the spartan, high-tech compartment, where red EMERGENCY! DO SOMETHING! lights blinked on every panel.

"Got a little trouble here, feller," Suggs explained. "That dang Hondu deck-swabber tried to take command, didn't want me to take the necessary action, like all them idiot lights is saying I got to." Suggs returned his attention to the console before him, resumed setting up a complicated sequence of relays. Retief studied the pattern, then stepped in and quietly threw in the Master Override switch. Suggs grabbed, but Retief pushed his arm aside.

"Just what do you have in mind, Captain?" he asked.

"Jest like you see, feller," Suggs snapped. "And don't go messing with my command, here. Got serious work to do."

"What you're laying out there will overload the converters," Retief told him. "And one of them already has a fake meteoroid stuck in it."

"Sure," Suggs agreed readily, then: "Whattaya mean, 'fake'? How'd you—?"

"It's burned as if it had made a fast passage through a dense oxygen-rich atmosphere," Retief elaborated. "But we're in space, well above the argon exosphere of Stug. Somebody who had only seen meteorites in a museum on Terra, and didn't know how they got full of pits and holes, faked up a slab of industrial nickle-iron to fit his idea of a piece of space-debris."

"Dumb," Suggs commented unemotionally. "But they got to get up pretty early in the afternoon to sting Calvin Suggs, Captain, SMM (Reserve)."

"Why blow the converters?" Retief persisted.

"Can't you see, feller?" Suggs demanded. "It's the only way to like thwart whatever scheme somebody got in mind."

"When you cross-link the converters," Retief stated, "you'll blow off the aft half of the ship."

"Durn right," Suggs confirmed, contentedly. "Better to scuttle my command than to have her took over by pirates or hijackers, or trash like that.

And as long as I'm all the way forrad, it's no fuze off my rockets."

"What about the four hundred diplomats and their staffs you have aboard?" Retief queried.

"Some of 'em might survive," Suggs suggested indifferently. "Them's strange diplomats," he went on. "Always thought diplomats was nice, perlite fellers in striped pants, but I got about two hundred o' the four hundred pulling rank and tryna take over my command, even that green deck-ape."

"The various delegations naturally include the Ambassadorial staffs," Magnan explained, poking his head in, "including their military advisors and technical people, some of whom, as you observed, are less than gracious in their manner."

"Won't be hardly no loss to blow 'em to Kingdom Come," Suggs summed up. "Step aside, there, feller!" He reached for the big, white EXECUTE lever. Just then Retief heard a distressed bleat from Magnan. He stepped outside the CD to help his badly shaken colleague inside.

"It—it moved!" Magnan whimpered. "I distinctly saw that nasty corpse move its arm."

"I ain't no corpse, bub," the Hondu's bass voice rumbled from below. Magnan leaped back as the wounded deck-swabber clambered up into view. The big spacer paused to wipe yellow-brown blood from his viridian eye and onto the bulkhead. "Lousy little runt snuck up behind me," he grumped. "Give me a sprongache that's got 'Jazreel' wrote all over it, or like that." He thrust Magnan aside.

"What *you* doin up here in capn's country, Terry?" he demanded.

"I came up to ensure that no unauthorized personnel attempted to intrude here," Magnan told him stiffly.

"That's a hot one," Gloon grunted. "You're unauthorized personnel your ownself."

"Hardly," Magnan contradicted sharply. "I assure you that under the circumstances, my presence here is not only appropriate but mandatory; check FSR 1-923-b, if you like."

"Happens I *don't* like, Buster," Gloon said discouragingly. "So if you're authorized like you claim, who authorized you, hah?" He thrust his blood-smeared face close to Magnan's and bared his square, chartreuse teeth.

Retief took him by the shoulder and spun him around to face him. "I did," he told the astonished fellow.

"Yeah? And who are you supposed to be?" the eight-foot Hondu sneered. He reached as if to push Retief aside, then *whoof*led and bowed from the waist.

"Sneaky," he wheezed. "I never seen no cargo-ram."

"Life is full of trifling disappointments," Magnan put in from behind the big fellow. "Now you'd best betake yourself below before I become annoyed."

"Geeze, we can't have that, can we, mister?" the Hondu replied in an attempt at an insouciant manner, spoiled by his sudden yell and grab for support before plunging headfirst down the narrow companionway.

"Retief!" Magnan gasped. "You didn't trip him!"

"Nope," Retief replied cheerfully. "You did—he fell over your foot. I only pushed him."

"If he should strike his already wounded head

on those steel treads . . ." Magnan started. "I shudder to contemplate—"

"Right," Retief confirmed. "Don't think about it. As you pointed out, ochre and vert are a tasteless combination." He broke off to step back inside in time to seize Suggs as he was about to unlock the board. As Magnan shrank back, Retief tossed the captain down on top of Gloon, eliciting sharp yells from both. He pulled Magnan inside and dogged the hatch shut.

"All right, Swabber Gloon!" the squawk-box rasped. "I see by the repeater panel here you got the CD secured."

"It's Kouth!" Magnan gasped.

"Now, I'm depending on you, Chief Gloon," Kouth went on, "to set this here bucket down nice and easy on Old Moon, right dead on the target like I shown you onna chart."

"Hard lines, Mr. Kouth," Magnan said to the squawker. "I have determined that it is upon Mr. Retief and myself that the responsibility devolves to take control of this vessel. And we intend to take the necessary action to safeguard the lives and property of the passengers, as well as the vessel itself, for the safe return of which ITCH is responsible."

"You must of slipped yer moorings, Cull," Kouth came back. "If I gotta come up there—" he paused. "By the way, whereat's that Swabber Gloon I dispatched to he'p the Cap'n?"

"He fell down," Magnan supplied crisply. "And I venture to predict that if you should attempt to intrude here, you yourself might encounter the same unfortunate slippery spot."

"Frankly, Retief," he added *sotto voce* behind

his hand, "I trust that Mr. Kouth less at every encounter."

"Very perceptive of you, sir," Retief congratulated his supervisor. "But this class of vessel requires at least two people to maneuver it; one up here and one aft in the Power Section, and I don't think we can count on Chief McCluskey for cooperation."

"Probably not, the cheeky fellow," Magnan agreed thoughtfully. "In fact, I think it is incumbent upon me to report him to Captain Suggs—or it would be if you hadn't thrown that officer away."

"I'm sorry to say it was necessary," Retief told Magnan. "He was intent on blowing us all up."

"Shocking," Magnan remarked, and paused. "But do you realize what this means? One of us has to return aft and do whatever is necessary."

"Quite correct, Mr. Magnan," Retief confirmed. "Unless we can recruit someone from among the naval attaches aboard."

"Dream on, Terry," Kouth's gravelly voice broke in. "Youse Terries—yeah, I reckernize youse—are gonna like roo the day youse tryda muscle in on Jerry Kouth's operation."

"Let's go aft, Mr. Magnan," Retief proposed. "Our orbit is decaying, and we're going to be in thick atmosphere and start breaking up in another ten minutes."

"Then let us by all means make haste!" Magnan ordained. Retief undogged the hatch and they went down, stepping over first Gloon, then at the foot of the steep steps, Suggs, who groaned and muttered: "I can hear atmospheric molecules whanging off the hull already. We got to hurry up here. You need a reliable boy aft, gents, and I volunteer, if I

can get up. You sprained my moobie-bone, feller,"
he told Retief aggrievedly, as the latter helped
him to his feet.

"Better get back there and give Chief McCluskey
a hand," Suggs rattled on. "Seems like he done
gone sour on me," he added as he staggered away,
pounding his ear with the heel of his hand.

"Can we depend on him?" Magnan asked dubiously.

"Not a chance," Retief dismissed the idea. "But
we can send someone back to keep an eye on
him."

"Grand Captain Blance," Magnan suggested
gloomily. "No doubt he's ranking naval officer
aboard."

4

From one deck above, the continuing disturbance
in the Grand Salon was audible. Non-Terran voices
boomed, squeaked, shrilled and rasped, all, it
seemed, claiming primacy.

"No one's doing anything constructive," Magnan
moaned. "While they should be putting their heads
together to save the ship, they're wrangling over
who's to be in command of the derelict when it
disintegrates. Absurd!" He pushed ahead into the
salon, where the din was like a storm at sea. A few
voices rose above the tumult.

". . . got my commission right here!" a tall,
purple Rikk was yelling.

"My date o' rank goes back to when you were
getting your first GI gill-trim!" countered a pancake-
like Jaq warlord in copper bangles.

"—protocol!" an insignificant-appearing Zub from Quopp shouted.

"To natter of protocol in the face of my over-whelming credentials as Great Hivemaster of Yan!" a Groaci diplomat protested in a penetrating whisper.

"That's Shoss, a mere Assistant Military Attache," Magnan observed.

"Correction, Mr. Magnan," Retief countered. "That's Colonel Hivemaster Shoss, brevet Lieutenant-General, one of Groaci's most-decorated troublemakers."

"To have heard that, Retief!" the Groaci hissed, turning on the Terrans, his distended throat-sac a deep purple, indicating Extreme Wrath, Righteous, (B-52). "In your profound ignorance of noble Groacian tradition, you grossly mis-translate the proud honorific 'Thusfoth,' which in fact might better be rendered 'Trusty Rectifier of Egregious Wrongs' rather than 'Troublemaker,' as you so crudely suggested. I outrank a Troublemaker First Degree by nine grades!"

A preternaturally tall, long-beaked Quornt in stained fatigues without rank badges thrust Shoss aside. "I'll put it to you gents," he told Magnan. "Who ranks, a Maker of Ritual Grimaces First Class from some third-rate power, of a Quornt All-Conquering Annihilator of Hostile Armadas?"

"It's a toss-up," Retief advised him.

"So, OK, I'll toss him up," the Quornt acceded contentedly, and turned to grab an ornately-dressed Frib and throw him carelessly aside.

Magnan made an abortive lunge to intercede, but met a horny knee to the jaw, and stumbled aside, muttering, almost inaudibly:

"You fail to understand the intent of my subordinate's proposal."

"Better tone it lower, feller," the Quornt advised. "Keep it inaudible and I can't hardly take offense at what I can't hear, right?"

"Possibly," Retief said, as he stepped hard on the tall creature's unpolished boot and kicked him hard on the knee, causing him to jerk futilely at his trapped foot and then topple backward, arms windmilling, to impact the floor with an impressive *whoomp*!, knocking the cocked hat from the pointy head of a Zanubian admiral in the process. The admiral uttered a hoarse yell and drew his ceremonial sword, which Retief confiscated for safekeeping.

"Mutiny!" the disarmed flag officer bellowed.

"Whatever you say, Admiral," a Zanubian Lieutenant Last Class replied, and knocked him down. The melee spread rapidly, heated conversation turning to inept fisticuffs in a trice.

"Good lord," Magnan mourned. "Heated conversation has given way to inept fisticuffs in a trice!" He broke off abruptly as two heavy-set aliens, identical even to their thick mops of head-tendrils except that one was bright orange, the other blue, locked in a complicated wrestler's grip and counter-grip nearly ran him down.

"Gloian and Blort, pursuing their fratricidal competition even here, in the halls of diplomatic sweet reasonableness!" The shaken First Secretary and Consul exclaimed. "Why, I do believe that's General Barf—you remember the general, Retief. Really a most reasonable chap, once he gets past that lamentable tendency to strafe first and negotiate afterward."

"What's to negotiate?" the general demanded, at the same time attempting to dislodge his adversary's gouging digit from his sensitive zatz-patch. "You think I'm gonna yield pride of place to this here Blort? Not broody likely!"

"But—he's a fellow native of Plushnik!" Magnan protested. "I should think—"

"Right!" Barf confirmed, "preferably before you talk! And I ain't no native! I got shoes on same as you, fancypants!"

"Retief!" Magnan mourned. "What's a Deputy Chief of Mission to do? They're incorrigible! Look at that great ugly Nether Furthuronian molesting that poor, pacifist Grotian. I think that's poor dear D'ong, isn't it? Why doesn't she whaffle, I wonder?"

"That would be cowardly in the extreme, Ben," D'ong reproved, even as she eluded the Furthuronian Primary War Chief by deftly extruding a flexible member ending in a large, knobby fist, with which she stunned her aggressive tormentor with a sharp rap to the barf-node. She stepped aside as he fell heavily.

"Pity to resort to violence," she commented, "but these Yahoos leave one scant choice."

" 'Yahoos'?" Magnan gasped. "My dear Madame Secretary—these are the cream of the Arm's career diplomats, chosen by their respective peoples as delegates to a tribunal which will establish peace in the Galaxy for a millennium at the least!"

"If the fate of the Galaxy depends on this bunch agreeing with each other," D'ong commented, "maybe I'd best whaffle after all. Do pass along my regards to dear Freddie." With a sharp *whap*! of imploding air, she disappeared.

"I give up," a bristly pink Spism declared loudly,

and bustled to the fore, its wiry arms overhead. "I saw you vaporize old D'ong, which she wasn't a bad old dame, for a Grotian! Leave me live, and I won't say a word."

"You may relax, Mr. Ambassador," Magnan soothed the excited fellow. "I assure you I did not 'vaporize,' as you put it, her Excellency the Ambassador of Grote!"

"We're not, after all, blind, Ben," the Quornt Annihilator cut in harshly, brushing himself off after his fall. "I myself was assaulted but now by your assistant," he added, then turned to address the crowd whose scuffling members had paused in mid-attack at what they had taken to be the sound of a hardshot.

"Clearly," the tall warrior called, "we are victims of an insidious Terry plot. Was it not haughty Terra which proposed the Convention of this Tribunal? It seems we are to be done away with, one by one, whilst our attention is distracted by the petty disputes so cleverly fomented by none other than Ben Magnan and his notorious tool, Retief!"

"Yeah, I was just saying—" someone shouted. And "I seen him, too!" another contributed.

"Where's Mr. Kouth?" a hoarse voice yelled from the far side of the salon, at once seconded by a chorus of demands for Boss Kouth.

"It just might be expedient at this point," Magnan whispered to Retief, "to take a leaf from D'ong's book and whaffle. You do recall the technique, I hope?" So saying, he squeezed his eyes shut and a second *whap*! sent the close-pressing onlookers back a step, setting off a brisk renewal of the free-for-all. Retief made his way through the press, fending off random blows and charging combatants as he went. Suddenly Kouth appeared directly in his path, planted solidly and blocking the way. He looked at Retief without visible joy.

"OK, where's that tricky side-kick o' yourn?" he demanded. "I wanna talk to him."

"Oh, he must be off somewhere minding his own business," Retief told the ill-tempered Boss.

"Is that some kinda crack?" Kouth inquired.

"Not unless you feel *you're* not minding your own business," Retief told him.

"Yer too smart-mouth fer yer own good," Kouth stated. "Who are ya, anyway? Some kind big general, that pal o' yours said, but I ast around, and seems like you're only one of these here Embassy Johnnies. So how about it?"

By this time Kouth's variegated retainers, many in crew uniform, had formed a loose circle around the two.

"As it happens, Mr. Kouth," Retief said calmly, "I'm not on active duty in a military capacity at this time."

"Oh," Kouth mimed surprise, grinning around at his strong-arm squad. "He ain't on active duty," Kouth sneered. He returned a threatening, gimlet-eyed gaze to Retief.

"Yer a little too active to suit me," he announced in a tone he seemed to feel was intimidating, at the same time rolling his well-developed shoulders and opening and closing the large fists that hung at his side. He brought one up in what was intended to be a deceptively lazy motion, and scratched above one badly twisted ear with a loud rutching sound, then whipped his hand, flat now, over and down in a whistling arc which ended in a sharp *smack*! as Retief casually caught the wrist and held it. Kouth tugged; Retief held firm. Kouth tried to twist his arm free, and Retief added to the torque, forcing the aggressive Boss to his knees. There was a mutter from his retainers. Retief jerked Kouth to his feet.

"Say 'I was a bad boy' three times," Retief ordered, bending Kouth's hand back until his wrist made popping sounds.

"I was a bad boy three times," Kouth gobbled. "Now lemme go, before—"

"Yes," Retief inquired interestedly, and gave him another two degrees of over-extension.

"Before you break my arm," Kouth amended, then, catching the eye of someone to Retief's right, added: "And I hafta get tough!"

Retief reached over and caught the man on his right by the hair, as the latter ducked his head for a charge. Retief jerked him close and shifted his grip to lay his forearm across the fellow's cheekbone, and levered upward slightly, eliciting a terrified squawk from the would-be attacker.

"Yer running outa arms," Kouth muttered, and tried a snap-kick, which met a boot-sole to the shin. Kouth groaned and lunged backward, as two more of his boys closed in. Retief jerked Kouth to the left, swinging him in an arc which lifted the Boss's feet from the floor; the flailing members knocked the foremost man back among his fellows. Then Retief lifted the other man by the head, as Kouth was led off, bleeding from the mouth, by his solicitous allies, one of whom produced a snub-nosed hard-shooter and aimed it at Retief, who kicked it from his hand.

"Nicely did, pal!" a Furthuronian Marine Guard Sergeant commented, neatly catching the slug-gun on the fly. "I been meaning to speak to this Boss Kouth my ownself about his manners, which he ain't got any. So, you taking over now, or what?"

"I defer to his Eminence," Retief said graciously, inclining his head toward the Hoogan Cardinal in full canonicals who had come over to see what was going on.

"You mean you're backing down to some kinda sissy preacher?" the Furthuronian demanded in a tone of Astonishment at an Unprecedented Shift in Strategy.

"It's more of a tactical play, Clarence," Retief told the multi-tentacled, slug-like non-com. "This is Cardinal Oh-Moomy-Gooby, a redoubtable warrior in the cause of Church reform and tax-free booze."

"Sounds like a all-right guy, all right," Clarence conceded and faded back.

"In the absence of any further pretenders to the mantle of Captaincy," the Cardinal intoned, "I shall accept the responsibility." That settled, His Eminence withdrew to a shadowy alcove and his brandy bottle.

"I wun't take that too serious, pal," Kouth offered, mumbling through his bruised mouth. "The old boy will be busy with his sauce fer awhile, and then he'll be so juiced he won't have no more big ideas about commanding no ten-thousand-tonner. So I'll jest step into the breach like they say, and ease her down nice on Old Moon."

"Not quite," Retief corrected the Boss. "I'm putting her down on Stug, as scheduled."

"You still on that kick, feller?" Kouth inquired as if amazed. "I already tole yer I and my boys are giving the orders now, and that's it." He broke off to yell, "Hey, Charlie!" to which responded a small, unshaven Terran in incredibly soiled whites, to the sleeves of which three shiny gold stripes had been stitched so hastily that Charlie was kept busy tucking the loose-flapping ends back in place.

"Yessir, Mr. Boss, sir," Charlie panted, offering a salute which resembled a wave of farewell to a departing traveler.

"This here," Kouth said importantly, "is Cap Stunkard, got more years in space than most has hours. He's my First Mate."

"Do you mind if I look at your captain's papers, Captain?" Retief inquired.

"Look ahead, if you can find 'em," Stunkard agreed carelessly.

"Mr. Kouth," Retief addressed the Boss again, "You and all your adherents are under arrest. Go lock yourselves in your quarters."

"Me?" Kouth echoed, trying for Astounded at Unparalled Impertinence, Level Four. "And whattaya mean 'my derents'? I ain't got none, nor no butterfly collection neither. Charlie, you got yer orders. Do it!"

Charlie took a brisk step to comply, but rebounded from the arm Retief had thrust out across his path. Charlie cast a dubious look at Kouth, then set about applying various Yug-Sub-Woo holds to the obstacle until Retief flipped him aside. "Now," he told Kouth, "don't wait for a police escort." He gripped Kouth's shoulder and spun him to face the aft grand passage. "Will you walk, or shall I throw you?" Retief inquired in an interested tone.

"Naw, naw, nothin like that, pal," Kouth hastened to blurt. "I was jest going down thataways."

He set off, reassembling his dignity as he went, pausing momentarily to confer hastily with various of those who had been vigorously seconding his self-nomination, each of whom faded back and began working his way toward Retief.

"Mind your flanks, Retief," the Fustian elder, Whelk, suggested from his place on the sidelines. "May I have the tall ugly one with the bread-knife?"

"Certainly," Retief agreed. "Don't spoil him for the trial, though."

Whelk moved off, as ponderous as a walking crane, and Retief watched as Kouth hastened off along the passage toward passenger country. Suddenly he halted, spun and raced back toward the salon.

"Look out!" he yelled. "They're coming!" Most of the contentuous crowd fell back in alarm, while the others rushed forward to comfort their leader.

"It's the blue Cobblies!" Kouth shouted hoarsely. "We ain't got a chancet!"

"Calmly, now, everyone," Cardinal Gooby's resonant voice boomed out. "You, there, Admiral! And you too, General Blow! I'm surprised at such intemperate behavior in officers of your respective ranks. Keep calm! Blue Cobblies, indeed! All enlightened beings are aware that the term is a reference without a referent, applying as it does to mere figments of superstition!"

"Yeah, maybe," a shaken ambassador from Icebox Nine offered. "But them figments are swarming all over the place! See for yourself!"

The Cardinal, ignoring the jibe, wrapped himself in his robes and sank back into meditation. The salon was cleared now of passengers, except for those flattened against the walls, and one other, the gorgeously caparisoned Grotian Ambassadress D'ong.

"Oh, Retief," she called. "I do hope you don't mind my meddling, but it *did* seem an appropriate moment to boggle; dear Ben seemed *so* upset!"

Just then Magnan appeared from a door marked PRIVATE—AUTH PERS ONLY. He paused to glance about the vast, abruptly silent salon, frowned, and hurried across to Retief.

"Oh, there you are!" he caroled. "I do hope you weren't alarmed when I whaffled so abruptly. Actually, I wasn't sure I still remembered the technique; that's why I just nipped over to D'ong's cabin to confer with her; it was her idea to boggle; and it seems to have worked wonders. Astonishing how very sophisticated people believe in blue Cobblies when they see them advancing in full cry!"

"I'm glad you came to me, Ben," D'ong told Magnan when the latter had concluded his briefing. "Surprised, too," she added. "But I'd have assumed you'd whaffled to the planetary surface, to inform our hosts of the reason for the delay."

"Hardly," Magnan huffed. "One doesn't leave one's colleagues in the lurch, while one retreats to a safe haven, however logical one's rationalization might appear."

"Pray accept my apologies, Ben," D'ong pled earnestly. "I meant to impute no baseness to you."

"Of course," Magnan reassured the sensitive Ambassadress. "As for your blue Cobblies, I think it's time to just boggle them back where they came from, before they drive all these fine diplomats to distraction."

"It's not quite so simple as that, Ben," D'ong

told him. "You must recall that a considerable adjustment to the vorb plane is necessary to effect such a wide-scope illusion. I fear my vital energies are too depleted now to reverse the effect."

"You mean?" Magnan yelped.

D'ong nodded a head she had deployed for the purpose. "But perhaps if you'd join with me, Ben . . ."

"Of course," Ben agreed at once. "But I'm not at all sure I know how."

"It's quite simple," D'ong reassured him. "I'll show you."

"Hey, Cap," Kouth blurted, staggering up to the threesome, "whattaya doin about these here like blue Cobblies and all?"

"Shocking!" Magnan retorted. "Now that an *unexpected* disaster rears its head, suddenly you're demanding that the very person whose credentials you rejected produce a remedy. Why don't you and your minions deal with the trifling annoyance yourselves?"

"Ain't none of my boys ever seen anything like 'em before," Kouth complained, "cept Woozy, o' course; he's so far gone on the pink stuff he seen everything, but all he can do is climb the drapes and yell *I see 'em!* No help there."

"What do these Cobblies of yours look like?" Retief asked the badly shaken Boss. Kouth's jaw dropped.

"You got bad eyesight or somethin, Cap?" he demanded. "How you gonna clear 'em outa here if you can't even see 'em?"

"The entities you see, sir," D'ong put in, "have no substantive existence: they represent your own neuroses objectivized. To no two persons do they appear the same. Since Mr. Retief is remarkably non-neurotic, the phenomenon fails to affect his optic nerves."

"Oh, yeah?" Kouth came back. "I ast Little Harry, and he seen the same as me: like little flat worms, with shredding hooks all over, coming on in a solid wave. They're right there, see?" He pointed to a bare spot on the floor six inches from his ankle. "You telling me they ain't?" he demanded and raised a boot to stamp hard on the floor. "Got the sucker!" he cried happily. "OK, everybody," he called, as he turned and strode out into the middle of the deserted floor. "Let's get 'em!" he ordered. "You, Stan, just stamp on 'em!" He began clapping his hands rhythmically. "Everybody dance!" he yelled, and proceeded to bawl out the words to a hillbilly lament. People were stirring, jittering, stamping, and in a moment the room was a sea of wildly bouncing beings. The band, caught up in the frenzy, deployed from their refuge behind the bandstand and struck up in approximate accord.

"Good lord," Magnan moaned. "It's like a convention of St. Vitus' Dance victims." As he spoke, he began to bob erratically, then took a tentative step, and followed it with an entire series of quick hops, until D'ong extruded a tentacular member and caught his arm, stilling him. "Ben," the shy Ambassadress said, tugging Magnan back to her side. "Doubtless it's excellent therapy, but we must exert ourselves to dissipate the hallucination, not reinforce it."

"To be sure," Magnan agreed happily. "But they *do* squish so delightfully! Besides, I haven't cut a rug in years!"

"The situation is deteriorating, Retief," D'ong

muttered. "We can't let it get out of hand; could you bring Ben back to his senses, do you suppose?"

Retief said, "I'll try," and stepped to Magnan's side. "If Ambassador Spoilsport saw you cutting the rug," he told the restless First Secretary, "while *he*'s struggling to keep our hosts engaged in light chit-chat to divert their attention from the fact that the members of ITCH have failed to appear for the conference *he* persuaded them to tolerate, I think your interest in terpsichore would vanish in a hurry."

Magnan went rigid for a moment, then relaxed and hastily ducked behind D'ong.

"I don't know what came over me," he started. "Do you really think the gimlet-eyed old devil was looking? Heavens, I knew he had his spies planted everywhere, but *here*, aboard ship?"

"There, there, Ben," D'ong soothed, turning to embrace him with a hastily improvised comradely arm. "No one saw you except Retief and myself, and a remarkably graceful figure you cut, too, indeed! But now we have work to do. Just cinch up the old sphincters nice and tight, and . . ." her voice dropped to a whisper. Magnan was nodding hesitantly, then eagerly.

"Yes, yes, of course I can do it!" he cried. "Nothing simpler!"

"We have to link arms, remember," D'ong continued as Magnan closed his eyes in concentration. He nodded vigorously and took D'ong's temporary arm. A moment later, the music stopped with a crash, only Kouth's off-key voice carrying on for a moment:

". . . but I didden cheer nobody prayy. . . ."

"In that connection," the booming voice of Cardinal Gooby cut through the hubbub, "as the direct representative of the vicar of God, I of course outrank any mere temporal authority. Accordingly, I have decided to put an end to this foolish disputation once and for all. It is to *me* that you may come for your instructions. Ah, Retief," the Prince of the Church added in a lower tone. "Since I have little practical experience of the operation of deep-space passenger vessels, I appoint you to the post of Advisor in that sphere. What, for example, should I do now?"

"Actually, Your Eminence," Retief told the imposing church-being, "We no longer have much choice. Do you hear that whistling sound?"

"Ah, now that the cacophonous ensemble has discontinued its efforts," the Cardinal commented, nodding, "I do indeed hear a most unpleasant screeching. It seems to be coming from all directions. What is it?"

"We've lost velocity and dipped into the atmosphere," Retief told the massive being. "So we're committed to putting down on Stug."

"Here, we cain't do that!" the runty Stuggan named Little Harry blurted. "Let's jest see what Boss has got to say about this!" He darted away.

"It appears," Magnan told the excited Kouth when he appeared moments later, loudly objecting, "that you are presented with the *fait accompli*. We're committed to landing. So you may as well lend a hand to help us get down intact."

"OK, onney first I wanna be sure nobody don't hole *me* responsible. Jest write out a free pardon or like that, letting me and my boys, too, off the hook, for any crimes we might of did."

"I fear that will not be possible, Mr. Kouth,"

Magnan told him distantly. "Still, if you wish to survive you'd best pitch in. Now be about it."

An undernourished fellow with a worried frown came up and Kouth caught him by the arm and conferred briefly with him. Magnan caught the name "McCluskey." The fellow hurried away.

"OK, gents, sure, I'll save yer bacon for youse," Kouth grated in a sudden attempt at a gracious manner. "Jest wait a minute till Stan gets back . . ."

"Wherever has that ruffian, Gloon, betaken himself?" Magnan queried, peering around anxiously. "He's an experienced spacer, so perhaps we'd better send him aft to man—or rather, to hondu the Power Section."

"Good idea," Kouth commented.

"I was not addressing my remark to you, sir!" Magnan snapped. "But to Mr. Retief. Retief! Don't you agree—"

"Certainly, sir," Retief replied. "I sent him back while you were tending Captain Suggs's bruises."

"But—without my permission—" Magnan blurted.

"Hardly, Mr. Magnan," Retief corrected him. "You suggested it yourself; it was simply a matter of timing—and so I expect to explain in my report."

"To be sure," Magnan agreed, nodding sagely. "It's what I had in mind all along."

"Well, gents, I got bears to shoot," Kouth put in absently. "I gotta run along. See youse in the slammer." Just then Stan returned at a lope, his close-set eyes looking more anxious than ever. He muttered in Kouth's ear.

"Whattaya mean, 'They ain't there'?" Kouth yelled. "I put 'em in there my ownself!"

"Pity about your arms cache, Kouth," Retief told the Boss quietly. "They fell into the converter."

"Oh, yeah?" Kouth snarled, at the same time hauling out from his under-jacket holster a snub-nosed needler.

"All except this one," Retief continued, and showed Kouth the heavy-duty crater gun; then he took the Browning from the Boss's hand and gave it to Magnan.

"Try not to shoot him unless perhaps you don't like the look on his face, sir," Retief suggested. Magnan took the weapon dubiously and tucked it away.

The whine of atmospheric molecules whanging off the hull had risen to a penetrating screech. People were covering their auditory organs and converging on Retief.

"You're the captain!" the Glorytian counsellor cried in a voice which rivaled the screech of reentry. "I *demand* you *do* something at once!" Her eye fell on Magnan.

"And *you*, you horrid little Terry! What are *you* doing to save innocent lives?"

Magnan drew his needler and pointed it at the Glorytian's sensitive zotz-patch.

"Shut up," he ordered quietly. "You, Madame," he went on, "are designated as chairman of the Tidying-Up Committee. Do something about this mess." He indicated the smashed glasses and spilled booze on every side.

"What committee?" the new appointee yelled. "I don't see no committee. And whattaya mean, telling me to shut up?"

"To be selected by yourself," Magnan clarified. "Now do be off about your business. This is a real gun," he added. "And while I should dislike to add to the mess, I will not tolerate any further vocalization from you. Scat!" he finished and jabbed the small weapon toward the gaunt female. She fled.

"Nice going, sir," Retief congratulated his colleague. "That voice of hers was precisely in resonance with one of the minor frequencies of the hull. Intolerable." He turned to Kouth, who was standing by with his mouth open.

"He'da *done* it," he muttered. "By golly, he'da done it, if she wouldn'ta shut up."

"Damn right," the blurry voice of the man called Woozy confirmed his chief's assessment.

Retief took Kouth aside and gave him his instructions. "And report to me on the bridge when you have everything ship-shape," he concluded.

5

Back in the Command compartment, Magnan wiped at his narrow face with an oversized floral-patterned tissue with the armorial bearings of the triarch of Gree, then noticed what he was using and quickly stuffed it into the waste slot as if to disassociate himself from the *lese majeste*.

"Heavens, Retief," he said, "however will you manage an already perilous approach, in a damaged vessel, without assistance from the crew?"

"Boss Kouth and his troops decided to help out," Retief told him.

"Oh," Magnan exclaimed, "I *don't* think I'd trust *him!* Though I did notice a number of his most vocal supporters scurrying about as if intent or something."

"There are a number of systems that have to be

set up manually," Retief explained. "Safety inter-locks to be set, for example, that are open for normal functioning."

"To be sure," Magnan murmured. "Now what? This panel looks so complex. Are you sure . . . . ?"

"I'm only sure," Retief said, "that if somebody doesn't do something, we'll break up in the atmosphere."

"Then by all means," Magnan blurted. "Can I help?"

"OK," Kouth's hoarse voice crackled from the talker. "I and my boys done like you said. Lucky fer you we're all experienced spacehands. Now what you got in mind?"

"Get up here at once," Magnan spoke up, "just as I distinctly heard Captain Retief tell you!"

"Keep yer lace britches on, Cull," Kouth admonished carelessly. "I'm onna way, ain't I?"

Retief quickly set up the panel for re-entry, first using a blast of reaction-mass to push the wounded vessel up and clear of the outer fringes of the Stuggan exosphere. The nerve-shredding whistling faded into inaudibility. Magnan heaved a sigh of relief. Carefully, Retief reduced the velocity of the hurtling mass that was the good ship *Expedient*, then gently eased her back down into the thin gas at the fringe of the soupy atmosphere below. The screeching resumed briefly, then became a deep-toned thrumming. Retief watched closely as the hull-temperature indicators crept up toward the fusing level of the outer ablative hull; then sheets of flame and an eruption of glowing particles were rushing past the look-out sensors. At last, dense air was reached and Retief deployed the airfoils, and the ship steadied into its long glide down.

Magnan stayed glued to the DV screens, watching the misty surface below as it slowly resolved into the mountains and plains, seas and rivers of the world known as Stug.

"I see Big Continent coming over the horizon!" he cried happily. "There's a town, too, just as it looks on the map back at Sector. Oh, boy! The port is north of the city, of course," he added, his voice fading as he recalled that Retief was a licensed space pilot and thus familiar with all major ports in the Arm.

"Won't his Excellency be delighted to see me right on time, too," Magnan burbled.

"I assume the question is rhetorical," Retief replied. "The last time Percy Spoilsport was delighted was when his rival for the post of Coordinator of the Academy for the Correction of Historical Errors fell into the sulphur pits at Yan and dropped out of the running."

"Yes, that was a stroke of luck for His Excellency," Magnan agreed. "Cecil Proudfoot was a fierce competitor. And as chief of ACHE, Spoilsport not only revised African history to eliminate all that horrid cannibalism and genocide, he was able so favorably to impress the Board of Examiners as to secure the additional plum as head of ITCH! A superb career plan, when he enticed poor Ambassador Proudfoot to go along on his PR tour of the Pits."

"It must warm the cockles of your heart, Mr. Magnan," Retief suggested, "to reflect that it is to this same gentle kindly man that you are about to report failure."

"Failure? I?" Magnan yelped. "How, pray, have

I failed? Why, simply to survive in these circumstances is itself an achievement!"

"We haven't actually survived yet, Mr. Magnan," Retief pointed out.

"Well," Magnan pulled at his chin. "I suppose not, not *quite* yet. Still, when I make my report to His Excellency we *shall* have survived. Wherein lies the failure there?"

"Don't you think he's likely to inquire into just who it was who poked a hole in ITCH's leased vessel, and why?" Retief asked casually, having first switched off the talker.

"Well, gracious, as to that," Magnan temporized. "I suppose the nosy old thing *is* likely to introduce some crude carping note into what should be an occasion of congratulation. But unfortunately we don't have any cogent answers to this unconscionable third-degree."

"We could ask," Retief suggested.

"Ask whom, pray?" Magnan came back sharply.

"We could start with Mr. Kouth," Retief suggested.

"I doubt he'll prove helpful," Magnan predicted. "The fact is," he went on in a confidential tone, "I shouldn't wonder if he isn't in some way implicated himself. Doubtless you noticed that most of the crew quickly leaped to support his tenuous claims to the abdicated laurels of Captain Suggs. Almost as if they had worked it all out beforehand."

"Good thinking, sir," Retief congratulated his chief. "So it seems he should be well qualified to shed some light on just what's going on here."

"Going on?" Magnan yelped. "Why, we're crashing in flames, that's what's going *on!*"

"I don't think that's any part of Kouth's plan,"

Retief corrected. "He didn't strike me as the kamikazi type, especially for no purpose."

"Still," Magnan sighed, "what Mr. Kouth is thinking is his secret."

"I still think we could ask him," Retief pointed out.

"Yes, I feared you'd think of that," Magnan said with a modest shudder. "I *do* so dislike mayhem . . ."

6

They found the Boss in the VIP lounge, sprawled at ease in a tump-leather throne intended for use by Heads of State only, surrounded by subordinates, most of them in the uniform of the Nine Planet Line, all talking at once:

". . . this here bucket into a viable mode, Boss," A cargo officer was saying urgently.

"—break up, and I mean soon!" a burly wiper insisted.

"Let 'em know fast, maybe we can do a eevee transfer or something," a plump fellow in chef's whites suggested half-heartedly.

"Easy, boys," Kouth cut short the babble. "Boss has got it all under control, right? Now, you, Stan, get back to yer Comm Section and raise Dooley on the tight-beam. I'll be along as soon as I finish my drink here." As he sipped from the tall glass in his hand, as if in response to his own command, his eyes fell on Retief, who had gently parted the circle of admirers, wounding four, to take a position in the front row. Kouth choked on his razzle-and-zizz-water and came to his feet in a lunge.

"Looky who's here, boys," he invited in a gleeful tone, then, to Retief: "I been looking for you, feller, which you don't quite get the program. Well, they don't call me Boss for nuthin, and I don't care a good rap what that shellback preacher says, I'm in charge here, and I say we still put her down on Old Moon. Any objections?"

"Only a few," Retief told him quietly. "For a start, there's the matter that unless someone takes the necessary action right now, this vessel won't be putting down anywhere. Then there's the trifling matter of four hundred diplomatic personnel aboard who expect to participate in a conference on Stug, not Old Moon, and that brings us to you. You're a loud-mouthed trouble-maker without enough brains to do a clean job of wrecking a space vessel for the salvage."

"Hey, Boss," Little Harry spoke up in the resounding silence that followed Retief's rebuttal, "you going to let this here civilian bad-mouth you like he done?"

"Not hardly, Harry," Kouth reassured the small man. "I'll fix his wagon right, but first I got to get back to Comm and talk to Dooley, down Old Moon." He pushed through his admirers a few steps, then halted and whirled.

"Whattaya mean, I din't do a clean job, wise guy?" he yelled.

"Not yet," Retief rebuked him. "We've still got the personnel to transfer, remember?"

"Why you think I'm talkin'a Dooley?" Kouth growled defensively.

"Why, the treacherous scoundrel!" Magnan contributed, ignoring Kouth's presence. "He intended all along to transfer himself and his vile cronies to safety, while the rest of us perished!"

7

When Kouth slammed into the communications section, startling a man who sat drowsing before the big panel, Retief and Magnan were close behind him.

"All right, Spike!" Kouth yelled. "I seen you sleeping on duty! Got a good mind to leave you ride her down!" He broke off as a great shudder racked the vessel.

"She's going!" he yelled, even louder. "Hurry yer dead butt up, Spike! Get Dooley on Number One, and I mean right now!"

"Already got him standing by, Boss," Spike told his excited leader. "Tole him ya wanned'a talk, soon's you give me the squawk!"

Kouth grabbed the shore talker. "All right, Dooley," he rapped out. "I guess you got the cattle-barge standing by like yer orders tole ya. So close fast and cover both hatches; we got to get out now. We're already on airfoils!" Even as he concluded his speech the ship bucked again, and an oblique pressure on boot-soles indicated that the hulk had taken up an off-axis spin.

"Won't be long now!" Kouth yelled. He jumped to the all-stations talker and ordered:

"All crew to abandon ship stations pronto! Secure the salon with all the marks inside! Do it!" he turned and for the first time realized that he and Spike were not alone.

"You heard me!" he shouted. "Go get locked in

the salon with the rest o' the losers!" He lunged toward Retief and met an oncoming fist to the jaw which loosened his knees and put a glaze on his eyeballs.

"Throw these here bums out, Spikey," he mumbled. "Watch the shrimp; he's mean as a fire-snake."

Spike rose dutifully and approached Retief. "I ain't leading with my chin like Boss, here," he told the bigger man, and set himself, then yelped as Retief spun him, grabbed him by the neck and crotch and upended him. Spike protested vigorously, but Retief stuffed him upside down into a narrow wall-locker, and turned to Kouth, who was draped, sagging, against the panel.

"Tell Dooley to make that two personnel barges," Retief ordered crisply. Kouth staggered a step and collapsed, snoring. Retief picked up the shore-talker and advised the dispatcher of the change in plan, ignoring the latter's yelp of protest.

"You expect me to pull another barge out'a my sock, or what?"

"Don't kid me, Dooley," Retief countered. "Just tell the flightline to rig Number Two for heavy cargo. Gold, in fact. The whole ITCH appropriation, in cash."

"Boy o boy," Dooley gobbled. "I guess you get a gold star on yer forehead after all, Boss! Hang loose. By the way, which part ya want us to match up with? That screen is showing three main pieces!" Kouth grabbed the talker and mumbled.

"Tell him the major fragment," Retief counseled. "No doubt she failed along the breakaway lines; she's still flying."

"The biggest one, dummy," Kouth told him. "Now get moving!" He dropped the talker and turned to Retief. "Hope yer satisfied, bub," he grunted. "I onney hope I tole him the right piece."

Magnan plucked at Retief's sleeve. "How do you know we're aboard the major piece?" he quavered.

"This is a Code Standard hull, Mr. Magnan," Retief reminded him. "It's stressed to give along the predetermined seams, and they're designed to keep the entire personnel core intact. I'm sure you'll recall the Code provision on that point?"

"To be sure," Magnan agreed, more confidently. "But it appears we'll all be firmly in the hands of these horrid pirates, once they board. We may as well forget the conference, I suppose."

"Too right, sport," Kouth spoke up. "Dooley ain't as good natured as me. Prolly be pretty pissed when he finds out we ain't got no load of gold guck aboard."

"Oh, but we have," Magnan corrected. "Just in case some of the members of the tribunal should prove recalcitrant, I, that is, Ambassador Spoil-sport, wanted to be sure to have cogent arguments available to bring the laggards into line."

"Bribes, eh?" Kouth queried respectfully.

"Hardly," Magnan sniffed. "It's called 'economic assistance.'"

"Good job it's here, anyways," Kouth commented contentedly. "But which piece is it on?"

"Right here, two decks down in the library, where miscreants of your stripe would never venture," Magnan told him smugly.

"What's that big word mean?" Kouth demanded. "Sounds to me like some kinda crack. Anyways, I read a book once. In reform school. All about the collapse o' civilization or something like that. Taken me all year, but I done it. Got a D on the test, too. Highest in the class. I ain't no dummy. So what say we sashay down and take a look. I ain't never seen no billion guck in cash before. Oh boy."

"Forget it, Mr. Kouth," Magnan advised the cocky fellow. "I've decided to lock you up right here in communications, first removing the master unscrambler disc, of course."

"And leave poor Spike and me to die, whilst youse skip out?" Kouth protested. "That there is krool, Mr. Magnan, is what it is. I guess Enlightened Galactic Opinion will have a word to say about that!"

"As it happens, Mr. Kouth," Magnan told the cheeky fellow, "I have no intention of informing EGO; nor, as it happens, of abandoning you to your richly-deserved fates."

"Oh, yeah?" Kouth countered truculently. "Uh, you mean you didn't plan to murder I and Spiky after all? See Spike," he addressed the locker, "I tole you he was a grand guy."

" 'Mean as a fire-snake' is, I believe, the term you employed," Magnan corrected tartly.

"I was onny kidding around-like, wasn't I Spiky?" Kouth appealed to his minion, whose reply was muffled by the steel door of the locker.

"Tell him to quiet down in there," Magnan ordered Kouth, who went over and muttered through the ventilation louvres in the panel. The pounding and yells subsided.

"Say, I almost forgot," Kouth spoke up brightly in the near-silence. "On account o' this here spin is making me space sick. I gotta go back to Power Section for my medicine."

"You needn't bother," Magnan told him. "I've already removed your arms cache, as I believe that fellow McCluskey has already advised you. Beside which, you must be airsick. We're in atmosphere now, you know."

"Figgered he was lying," Kouth confided. "Trynna pull a fast one."

"A great pity when one can't trust his own subordinates," Magnan commiserated. "But of course that's to be expected when one embarks on a career of crime; all one's associates are criminals."

"Same with diplomacy, I guess," Kouth offered sympathetically.

"A conscienceless criminal and a dedicated diplomat are hardly to be compared, sir!" Magnan rebuked sharply.

"Naw, I guess not," Kouth conceded. "We ain't got the scope o' your boys; you're the Big Leagues. But I guess we can get along OK anyways, right?"

There was a deep-toned *thump*! which added a new dimension to the off-center tumble of the derelict.

"That's Dooley!" Kouth blurted, and started for the door, shying as Magnan made a move.

"Just thought I'd check," Kouth explained contritely.

"We'll wait here," Retief told him. They did so, while Spike complained from the locker and the deck slowly precessed. All loose objects had gravitated to the aft outboard corner of the crowded compartment. Retief went to the big ground-talker unit, replaced the circuit-breaker and raised Stug Approach Control.

"Hey, what's going on out there?" an irritable voice demanded, almost blanketed in the static produced by the swarm of agitated particles in the midst of which the remains of the ship were slowly gyrating planetward. The buffeting and sounds of atmospheric friction were steadily increasing, amplified by the sounds of pieces tearing away from the disintegrating structure. "Looks like a meteor swarm," the controller resumed. "—that you, *Expedient?*"

"Say, there's two bandits on a closing course with you," the man on the ground said excitedly. "Might be some o' them wreckers plan to get a tractor beam on you and claim salvage rights!"

Just then, the closed-circuit talker linked to Old Moon came on line:

"Hard lines, Boss," Dooley's heavy voice came in loudly. "No can do. Seems like somebody forgot to do the annuals on the barges, the last few years, and they're grounded—prolly permanent. So you gotta get down the best way you can. Try for a nice solid impact here on Moon; we can smelt the gold out'a the remains later. Ta."

"The mug's tryna muscle me outa the picture," Boss Kouth growled. " 'Grounded', he says, and AC's got 'em on the screens ready to make contact!"

"Who'll be in command of the second unit?" Retief asked Kouth, who frowned and guessed:

"Prolly old Cuffs Dubois; useta be a line captain in the Bogan Naval Service."

"Raise him," Retief orderd; Kouth got busy with the intership gear and was rewarded with a thin, nasal voice saying:

"Right here, Boss," Dubois reported. "What's up? Dooley was all excited; said load all personnel— at first I thought he was abandoning the boys, here."

"Poor Dooley's not playing with a full deck," Retief told him. "We've got enough gold guck aboard to make every man rich, only we're in failure mode here. So get a beam on your lead barge, and then grapple onto the biggest piece of cargo-bay you can find. Over and out."

Kouth grabbed the talker and added: "We got a mutiny on our hands here, Cuffs; Dooley got a idear he can grab the whole take fer hisself. We'll fool him: hold him hard, like my, uh, aide here, Retief said, and set up a grapple to the port aft emergency hatch. Do it!" Then he used the PA to summon all crew to Emergency Stations—Plan B.

"—and we're gonna be boarded any second, by Colonel Dubois and his loyal crew," he concluded.

"Wrong, sucker!" Dooley's metallic voice cut across the squeals, whistles and rattles of the disintegrating vessel as he slammed into the compartment, a power gun in each fist. "I figgered you'd try something cute, Boss, so I got in here ahead of Cuffs and his traitors. Who's he think he is, tryna take his direct supervisor in tow?"

"Jest tryna give ya a hand, Dooley," Kouth alibied weakly. "See, we got a like little problem area here. We got to transfer all ship's complement to yer barge while we still got hull integrity here, so we got to move fast. My boys are all in place, ready to load."

The guns in Dooley's hands held steady on the Boss. There was a sudden outburst of thumping and yelling from the locker just beside Dooley; his eyes went to the source of the disturbance, and at the same moment, Magnan drew and fired the weapon he had tucked into his cummerbund; Dooley staggered back with a curse, dropping both guns so that his right hand could caress the left, ripped by the stream of small-caliber needles.

"I meant to tell you, if you wouldn't of been in such a big of a hurry," Kouth put in. "Watch this 'ere Mr. Magnan. He's a killer."

Retief thrust Kouth aside as he made a move for the fallen weapons and himself scooped them up.

"All right, Mr. Kouth," he told the frustrated Boss, "that's enough nonsense." Then he gave Kouth further precise instructions.

8

Half an hour later, after the diplomatic personnel had been herded, complaining bitterly, into the spartan accommodations of Barge Number One, and Kouth and Dooley and their respective cadres similarly crowded into the second scow, the last habitable section of the ill-fated *Expedient* fell apart and traced a spectacular arc of fire toward the uninhabited desert area fifty miles below. Magnan heaved a sigh.

"A sad conclusion to my mission," he moaned. "Whatever am I to say to His Excellency? Why, paying off the Statement of Charges for the ship alone will require the remainder of my active life."

"They'll have to promote you, sir," Retief suggested encouragingly. "You'll need the extra salary to keep up the payments."

"That's scant solace, I fear," Magnan retorted.

"When Ambassador Spoilsport and the committee learn that you have an entire barge-load of trouble-makers out of circulation and in tow, I'm sure that will outweigh the trifling loss of a time-expired contract hauler."

"Of course—with Boss Kouth and his gang of ruffians subtracted from the equation, agreement will be reached far more readily," Magnan cooed.

"I was thinking of the other barge," Retief told him.

9

With both barges safely if informally at rest on the ground of Interplanetary House, Retief and Magnan stepped out on the pale blue lawn and were intercepted at once by Nat Sitzfleisch, Recording Secretary to ITCH, who came up breathless. "There you are at last, Ben," he greeted the senior diplomat, ignoring Retief. "His Ex is furious. You've kept all these Stuggish big shots—ah—senior officials, that is, waiting, which they were far from enthusiastic about this gab-fest in the first place! Another five minutes and you'd have been late!"

Magnan gave Nat instructions as to the disposition of the bulky scows marring the formal gardens and, with Retief, proceeded up the broad walk to the imposing structure housing the deliberations of the select tribunal. After making their way through the crowded hallways where groups of attaches were gossiping excitedly, they were confronted by His Excellency Ambassador Extraordinary and Minister Plenipotentiary Elmer Spoilsport, whose expression reflected none of the more tranquil emotions.

". . . Captain Suggs is resting comfortably in

hospital, Magnan, as I'm sure you'll be glad to know," he announced excitedly. "He's not quite himself yet—keeps repeating the most extraordinary allegations regarding the proximate cause of his contusions—allegations in which your own name recurs with monotonous regularity—and by the way, there's a, ah, female counsellor from the Glory System, who has quite clearly suffered a breakdown—I hope! Says you actually menaced her with a Browning 2 mm! Under the circumstances I have no choice, of course, but to order you under close arrest, on your own recognizance, naturally, out of deference to your rank." He interrupted himself to gesture toward two large Terran Marines standing by. Magnan squeezed his eyes shut and appeared to be about to burst into tears. Instead, he smiled broadly, as Spoilsport bent his knees slightly, put his right foot forward in a jerky way, followed by his left, and exclaimed:

"Step on them—look at the vile things, Ben—! Wherever are they coming from? Rather a handsome shade of blue, though, one must admit." Then, as he leapt to left and right, stamping on the carpet, he began to sway from side to side and mutter.

". . . hunch yer honey out/hunch her in again . . . !"

"Mr. Magnan!" Retief commented admiringly. "You didn't tell me you'd learned to boggle."

KEITH LAUMER'S RETIEF

Adapted by Dennis Fujitake and Jan Strnad

© 1987 Laumer & Fujitake

MAD DOG graphics

COMES TO THE COMICS!

But don't look for *Retief* in the "Hey, Kids! Comics!" spinner at the supermarket. Our out-of-the-ordinary titles are available in comic book shops only! Check the Yellow Pages under "Bookstores" for the comic shop in your area, or send a *self-addressed, stamped envelope* to:

Keith Laumer's RETIEF
P.O. Box 931686
Hollywood CA 90093

**IF YOUR PLANET IS BEING EXPLOITED
BY CHITINOUS, TENTACLED MONSTERS
WHO THINK THEY OWN THE UNIVERSE,
WHO YA GONNA CALL?**

RETIEF OF THE CDT

Complete your collection of the irreverent adventures of the galaxy's only two-fisted diplomat, all by Keith Laumer with super series-look covers by Wayne Barlowe.

THE RETURN OF RETIEF	55903-6	$2.95	___
RETIEF'S WAR	55976-1	$2.95	___
RETIEF OF THE CDT	55990-7	$2.95	___
RETIEF AND THE PANGALACTIC PAGEANT OF PULCHRITUDE	65556-6	$2.95	___
RETIEF AND THE WARLORDS	65575-2	$2.95	___

Please send me the books checked above. I enclose _____ (Please add 75 cents per order for first-class postage and handling. Mail this form to: Baen Books, 260 Fifth Avenue, New York, N.Y. 10001.)

Name _____

Address _____

City _____ State _____ Zip _____

WE'RE LOOKING FOR
TROUBLE

Well, feedback, anyway. Baen Books endeavors to publish only the best in science fiction and fantasy—but we need you to tell us whether we're doing it right. Why not let us know? We'll award a Baen Books gift certificate worth $100 (plus a copy of our catalog) to the reader who best tells us what he or she likes about Baen Books—and where we could do better. We reserve the right to quote any or all of you. Contest closes December 31, 1987. All letters should be addressed to Baen Books, 260 Fifth Avenue, New York, N.Y. 10001.